Advance Praise for Sewing Holes

"With infinite grace, Sewing Holes explores love and loss, spirituality and crisis, redemption and forgiveness. …Read it, celebrate it, and buy copies for your friends, for this is a book that reminds us what the true nature of love is all about." ~ Connie May Fowler, author of *Before Women had Wings* and *How Clarissa Burden Learned to Fly*

"In her debut novel Sewing Holes, Darlyn Finch Kuhn has written an authentic and touching account of growing up in the 1970s that ties life in Jacksonville, Florida, to the national traumas of that era. … It's a generous tale of maturation that all young girls and their mothers and fathers should read. …" ~ Sena Jeter Naslund, author of *Ahab's Wife*, *Four Spirits*, and *The Fountain of St. James Court*

"In the tradition of Carson McCullers and Rick Bragg, Darlyn Finch Kuhn writes with an acute sense of romanticism, confusion and heartache that is childhood and family life in the American South." ~ Bob Kealing, author of *Calling Me Home; Tupperware, Unsealed;* and *Kerouac in Fl~~*

"With alternating doses of heartbr~ ' debut coming-of-age novel, Sewing Holes, ·offee and find a comfortable chair, becaus b you reading to the last line." ~ Julie Cc ~, Keep No Secrets, and *Rescuing Olivia*

"Darlyn, true to her adorable southern name, has spun a yarn that caught my heart like a mullet in a cast net. Sewing Holes has that southern way of turning tragedy into story … into love." ~ Stacy Barton, author of *Surviving Nashville: Short Stories* and *Like Summer Grass*

"…The young narrator's authentic southern voice, reminiscent of Will Tweedy in Cold Sassy Tree, *pulls the reader along a compelling journey of love, loss and redemption."* ~ Pat Spears, author of *Dream Chaser*

"Sewing Holes is a delightful debut novel that hits all the emotions. Highly recommended." ~ Terry Odell. author of the *Blackthorne, Inc.* and *Pine Hills Police* novels

Sewing Holes

by

Darlyn Finch Kuhn

Twisted Road Publications LLC

ISBN: 978-1-940189-08-6
Library of Congress Control Number: 2014955259

Cover Image by Tiffany Wolfe
Author Photo by Rich Johnson

Printed in the United States of America

www.twistedroadpublications.com

For Anita and Rachel ~ Before and After

Heartfelt thanks to:

Brad Kuhn, my husband and the love of my life, who inspires me to be a better writer and a better human being.

Rachel Finch-Bates, who never ceases to delight and amaze. So proud of the person you are; so grateful for the privilege of being your mother. And to Railan Bates-Finch, who makes my daughter happy.

Anita and Jack Cunningham, my loving parents, for your faith and support.

Robert Amos Lundin, Sr. and Jr., my father and brother, whom I will always love and miss, and will see again someday, in the life after this one. The Father, Son, and Holy Spirit, always.

Meschelle Kuhn, who allows me to practice unconditional love, and is growing to be a fine person, and to the extended Kuhn family, who tolerate my quirks with kindness because I make Brad happy.

All the members of the Jack Kerouac Writers in Residence Project of Orlando, especially Summer Rodman, Steven McCall, Janet and Geoff Benge, and Bob Kealing.

Connie May Fowler, who inspires through her love of the craft, the language, the magic of writing. This novel would not exist without her encouragement and coaching.

My writing group, the Pregnant Pigs, who saw the first stories that became Sewing Holes: Katherine Vaccaro, Kay Mullally, Terri Chastain, Renee Anduze, Karen Blondeau, Terry Odell, Julie Dunsworth, and Jill Yamnitz.

My professors at Rollins College: Philip F. Deaver (who made me believe I had a novel inside me), Susan Lilley, Lezlie Laws (Grammar Goddess, forgive my flaws), Bruce Aufhammer, Russ Kesler, Maurice O'Sullivan, Alan Nordstrom, Gail Sinclair, and Julie Cording.

My Holt School patrons: Thad and Polly Seymour, for the scholarship and their belief in me.

My professors at Spalding University's MFA program: Sena Jeter Naslund, Karen Mann, Kathleen Driskell, Katy Yocom, Molly Peacock, Roy Hoffman, Jeannie Thompson, Richard Goodman, Robert Finch, and Maureen Moorehead. Thank you for literally showing me the world.

The Scribblers: Mary Ann de Stefano, Jamie Morris, and Julie Compton (three beta readers who made this book better through honest feedback), Terry Godbey, Stacy Barton, Suzannah Gilman, Jim Crescitelli, Leslie Halpern, Eric Compton, Ed Masessa, Ilyse Kusnetz, Nancy Pate, Ruth Edwards, Diana Raab, and many others.

The folks at Siemens, who always believed, even when all I wrote were technical documents: Laura Holland (30 years of love) and Steve Holland, Christy and Aaron Peronto, Cristi and John Nemeth, Mary and Dave Chiozza, Mike and Lisa Hopkins, Milt and Starla McCarty, Bob Lowe, Frank Foulk, Kristine Kushner, Jad Jacob, Carlos Fabregas, Glenn Miller, John Matthews, Debra Tate, Sandy Bryant-Davis, Luda Kuzmich, Bill Marinara, Wendy Betts, and Leslie Dawson.

My teachers at Sherwood Forest and Harborview Elementary Schools, Highlands Junior High, and Ed White High School in Jacksonville, Florida, who fostered my love of books and of the South.

My grandparents, aunts, uncles and cousins, who all did the best we could with what we had. Love you all, here and gone.

My fellow authors on the Twisted Road: Sandra Gail Lambert, Pat Spears, Glenda Bailey-Mershon, Nance Van Winckel, and Susan Rukeyser. It is a privilege to be a Twisted Sister. What a ride!

And to Joan Leggitt, Founder and Editor of Twisted Road Publications, who makes dreams come true and improves everything she touches.

Sewing Holes

by

Darlyn Finch Kuhn

Memories are colored by perception,
and the truth is pocked with holes.
This is the way, after almost half a century,
I've stitched those holes together.

Prologue
Jacksonville, Florida, 1975

The day I tried to fix Mama started out like all the other days since Daddy died. In the morning I had a mother who was broken, but by nightfall I'd made things so much worse, she wouldn't even look at me. The fact that I did it for her own good made no difference. There are some wrongs that can't be made right, some mistakes that *sorry* can't make up for.

Why did I do what I did? I thought I had no choice.

I was fifteen, too old to sleep in the same bed with my mother, but in those first days after Daddy passed away, Mama needed someone to hold on to at night. I didn't mind, really, because it helped her get some rest. Sleep is a healing thing, and I wished I'd had more of it myself, but with my mother acting like she wanted to be in the cold ground more than she wanted to stay with me, slumber had a way of hovering just out of reach.

That night, Uncle Travis had just taken Suzie away and I had already crawled under the covers on what used to be Mama's side of the bed when she came in wearing her gingham nightgown, her wet hair wrapped in a towel. The tart-sweet smell of Dippity-Doo filled the room as she sat on the side of the bed that used to be Daddy's and curled her hair. Mama was thirty-eight and still slim, but looked older by the light of the lamp on her nightstand.

Grief added lines to her face; lack of sleep and frequent headaches traced dark circles under her eyes. I didn't have to glance past her into the mirror to know how much I looked like her, dark circles and all, though my hair, which I'd finally let grow from a pixie into a shag, was blonder than hers, and I had my daddy's dark brown eyes rather than her blue ones.

It felt nice to watch her work the icy green gel along each mousy-brown strand and secure them with bobby pins she drew from the quiver of pins held between her pursed lips. The tidy brown X's the pins made were like old times, because she hadn't curled her hair since the funeral. The bobby pins in her mouth kept her from talking, and that was fine with me. With the last hair slicked down and tamed, she wrapped her head with a pink satin scarf, to keep the goop off the pillow.

Mama shook a nerve pill into her palm from the plastic bottle on her dresser, then tossed it into her mouth and swallowed, without water. She padded to the bureau across the room and opened a drawer. I knew what she lifted out by the way she cradled them in her arms—the pale blue cotton pajamas my daddy wore when he went to the hospital to die. She sat down on the bed again and turned out the lamp, but by the streetlight shining through lace curtains, I saw her bury her face in the pajamas' soft folds. She cried without sound.

I put a hand on her shaking shoulder. "It's okay, Mama. I'm here."

She stopped crying, sniffled once, and dabbed at her eyes and nose with one sleeve of the pajamas. She stuffed them under her pillow and lay down, pulling the white eyelet bedspread up around her, taking my hand in hers. "It will never be okay, Honey."

I squeezed her hand, squinched my eyes closed, and prayed to no one in particular for her to go to sleep. After a while, her hand fell slack in mine, and her breathing grew deep and regular. Maybe tonight we'd finally both get a good night's sleep. The bed seemed to tilt and spin and I felt myself sliding toward slumber.

I thought I was dreaming when I felt Mama swing her legs over the side of the bed. The nightstand drawer slid open with a snick. What was she doing? I peeped out of one half-open eye and saw her lift something heavy and dark from the drawer. She put it into her lap, and stared at it.

I sat up and whispered, "What are you doing, Mama?"

Her head jerked toward the sound of my voice. Her face was a closed fist. She spoke, as if from far away. "Go to sleep, Honey."

She put the dark thing back in the drawer, and by the light from the streetlamp I saw that it was my daddy's pistol, which he'd always kept there in case of burglars.

She banged the drawer shut, lay back down, and closed her eyes. "Good night," she said, as if nothing had happened. Soon I heard the slow, steady breathing that told me Mama's pill had kicked in and she was asleep again. I stared wide-eyed at the ceiling.

The faces of Paw Paw, Kat, Suzie, and Daddy all swam in the dark above me. All four, inconceivably, gone. Jimmy, gone too, who knew where, and no help at all.

Mama was all I had left.

Mama, and the memories.

Part One

1970 – Five Years Earlier

One

A bell should ring when something important happens for the last time. Then you'd pay attention, and changes wouldn't sneak up on you. You'd be able to hear them coming. You'd get ready.

I was only ten and didn't realize it would be our family's last normal weekend. I had my nose buried in J.M. Barrie's book, *Peter Pan*, one Saturday morning when Daddy tiptoed into the den, glancing around the pine-paneled room and back over his shoulder into the kitchen. A bar with a chest-high pass-through separated the two rooms. "Honey," he whispered, "Where's your mama?"

I'm not sweet enough for my name, but Mama and Daddy didn't know that yet when they'd named me Tupelo Honey Lee, a decade earlier. My brother Jimmy had been in first grade and just learning to read back then. He found my first and middle names on the label of a mason jar in the Waffle House where the three of them had gone to eat dinner on New Year's Eve. I arrived in a great hurry before they could even get home that night, but thirty-four minutes too late to win the big stack of baby products that radio station WAPE awarded the first New Year's infant born in Jacksonville, Florida every year. There were no prizes for second place, as Mama liked to remind me.

"She's gone to the beauty parlor," I said. I was glad that, for once, Mama hadn't made me go with her to the stinky shop where she got her beehive hairdo fixed every Saturday. It was hot, noisy, and no fun for a kid who could not yet appreciate the sacrifices necessary to achieve the Southern standard of feminine beauty.

Daddy was short and muscular, his salt-and-pepper hair growing thin, his bald spot widening, but his brown eyes twinkled like a mischievous child's.

"Good!" he bellowed. Daddy reached into the deep left pocket of his khaki fishing pants, where he usually kept his harmonica, and pulled out a fat, shiny nail that looked about half the size of a railroad spike. From his right pocket he pulled a hammer, and with three powerful whacks, drove that nail right into the wooden support post that framed the doorway between the kitchen and den, at about his eye level.

"Mama's gonna pitch a hissy fit!"

Daddy didn't seem concerned at all. "She's pitched them before," he said. He patted his left front pants pocket, then his right, then patted each pocket again, looking perplexed. Reaching into the pocket of his blue T-shirt, he said "Aha!" and pulled out a shiny silver ring as big as my fist. He hung that ring on the nail he'd just pounded into the post.

Daddy turned back to me. "Honey-bunny, close your mouth before something flies in there, and hand me that bucket."

I looked where he was pointing, in the kitchen. "That old mop bucket?"

"That's the one."

I put down my book with a sigh, walked over and got the white plastic bucket, then set it down by the doorway where he'd hung the nail and ring.

"What are you doing, Daddy? Making something?" He loved to work with his hands, and could make almost anything he set his mind to.

"This is not just making something," Daddy said without a trace of a smile. "This is serious business." His hand disappeared again into the deep recesses of his fishing-pants pocket, and he pulled out a spool of fishing line, like he used with his rod and reel. Then he showed me a green plastic object shaped like a rocket ship.

"My needle," he announced.

"That doesn't look like any old needle I've ever seen."

"Sure is. It's for sewing holes together."

Daddy threaded the needle with the almost invisible fishing line.

He leaned down, rooted around in the empty mop bucket, and scooped up a handful of air, holding it aloft with a satisfied grin and wink. "Always start with a nice one," he said. With a flourish, he used the needle to fasten a loop of line onto the silver ring, tying a smart, tiny knot at each end of the loop. He tugged the line with one finger, and, sure enough, he'd sewn a "hole" to the base of the ring. He lifted me up by my waist so I could tug the line with my finger. Yep. He'd really done it.

"What are you making, Daddy?" I tried again, as he set me down with a grunt. I was small for my age, but still, I was no longer a baby.

He grinned. "Not sure. Might turn out to be something; might turn out to be nothing at all. Just have to wait and see." Then he reached into that bucket and scooped out another hole. "Oh, yeah," he said, measuring its heft. "That's a keeper."

He'd hooked me by then. After all these years, I don't recall how long it took Daddy to sew all those holes together, or even how many holes that old mop bucket held, but I do know that in no time at all I had pulled the footstool up close beside him, *Peter Pan* forgotten, and soon I was dipping into the bucket myself, hefting holes.

Daddy said it was easier on his back if I picked the holes out and handed them to him. A couple of times he scowled and made me throw a rotten hole out the door into the back yard. He was so disgusted by one that he took it into the bathroom and flushed it right down the john.

By the time Mama got home, looking spiffy and smelling of Aqua Net hair-spray, I'd forgotten about the big nail. But Mama always could find the cloud in any rainbow.

"James Lee, I Suwannee, this is why I can't have anything nice." Mama wouldn't say "I swear," even when you knew that's what she meant. She said swearing was a slippery slope leading straight to You-Know-Where. "What in the world do you think you're doing?"

Daddy dropped the needle, letting it dangle on the line while he grabbed Mama around the waist and kissed her on the mouth, three loud smacks.

"Welcome home, Yellow Rose of Texas," he said, as if she'd just fed him a spoonful of sugar. "M-m-m, you look good enough to eat." I noticed he didn't answer her question.

She pulled out of his arms, trying hard not to smile, and turned her attention to me. "I don't suppose you thought to tell him to stop nailing up the place."

I spread my arms and tried to look innocent. "There's no talking to him," I said, shaking my head. I'd heard her say that to my aunts, about Daddy, lots of times.

This time there was a definite twinkle in her eye as she made a *hmph* sound and stomped off to put her purse in her room. I grinned, because there was nothing I liked more than making Mama smile. I wanted more than anything for her to like me, even though most of the time I was sure she didn't.

Daddy and I didn't laugh as loud after Mama got home. She didn't care for a lot of noise inside the house. But we still worked quietly on his mysterious project.

As Daddy added row after row of lacy fishing line loops, Mama joined us in the den. She settled in at her sewing machine in the corner, with its view of Bass River, finishing up a new judo gi for Jimmy.

When that was done, she folded up the thick, heavy white fabric and set it aside.

"Honey, stop fooling around with that empty bucket and bring me your mending," she said.

I ran to my room and scooped up the small pile of drooping skirt hems, split-open jeans knees, and ripped arm-pits that seemed to magically grow on my desk chair. I loved climbing trees, and my wardrobe suffered for it.

I handed Mama the stack of mending and said, "It's not an empty bucket, Mama. It's just full of holes."

Mama snorted. "Like your daddy's head."

"You say that now, but wait till you see what I'm making," he replied.

I tried to guess what in the world it might be.

"Is it a spiderweb?" I asked, thinking of Charlotte and Wilbur.

He smiled and shook his head. "Nope."

"A poncho?" I guessed, and he laughed.

"Wouldn't keep you very dry, now, would it?"

"Is it an Indian dream-catcher, like we made out of string at Girl Scouts?"

He shook his head again.

Mama piped up. "Speaking of Girl Scouts, Honey needs to be sewing her new patches on her sash, not wasting time while I do all the mending. She could use the practice. Can't sew two stitches in a row the same size."

"She's not wasting time, she's helping her daddy feed the family," Daddy said.

Unless we were going to eat air sandwiches, his answer didn't make any sense to me, but I was glad he wasn't letting Mama make me sew, an activity she encouraged but I hated. I liked to do things I was good at, like the three Rs: reading, writing, and roller-skating.

"Mama, I'm going to be a newspaper reporter like Lois Lane when I grow up, so why do I need to learn to sew?" I asked.

"Yeah, and your brother's going to take the pictures, I know, I know. But who do you think sews Superman's britches when he rips them fighting Lex Luthor?" she asked.

Daddy laughed. "I reckon he patches them up himself with his X-ray vision."

"Spider-Man could spin some thread," I added.

Mama made a few remarks under her breath, but she didn't make me stop helping Daddy, so I stayed where I was and wondered why she always seemed to want to put me to work on something else whenever Daddy and I were having fun.

I didn't have any more good guesses about what he was making, and Daddy wasn't telling, so I worked real hard on my patience, and as the sun began to set over Bass River at the bottom of our hill, he took the hole-blanket down off the nail and held it up over his head by the silver ring.

"Stretch it out and let's see how big it is, Honey," he said. The sewn-together holes fell in poofy folds from Daddy's outstretched arm all the way down to the floor.

Jimmy arrived home from his part-time job at the gas station and came into the den to look, too, while I stood on the bottom loops to stretch Daddy's creation out tighter.

"Looks like Lady Godiva's wedding gown," said Jimmy, and we all laughed.

"Good guess," Daddy said. "He figured it out." He winked at me to let me know he was joking. Then he announced that his creation was "long enough" and reached back down into his bottomless pockets, pulling out small round silver weights he sewed onto the "hem" to pull the loops open.

Jimmy watched Daddy work, but wouldn't take another guess; he was sixteen and just wanted to look cool behind his mop of brown bangs. Anyway, I got the feeling he and Mama knew what the danged thing was and were just helping Daddy pull my leg. That happened a lot when you were the youngest in the family.

After Daddy finished sewing the weights on, he looped a long, slender rope through the top, and the four of us trooped into the back yard.

"Now I can practice," Daddy said.

I had reached the limit of my endurance for mystery. I didn't know whether to get mad, cry, or crawl between the stacked-up cement blocks that held up our house and pout. Under the house was a cool place to go when I needed to let off steam.

"Practice what?" I whined instead.

"Fishing," he said, with a reverence in his voice that I usually only heard when he said the blessing at dinner. "It's a cast net, for catching mullet at the beach."

Of course! I'd seen men fishing with nets before; I just hadn't put two and two together, since we'd started with a bucketful of air.

I thought he might head for Bass River, which ran behind our house, but Daddy tried the net out on our lawn first. He clasped one end of one fold of the mullet net between his teeth, and looped the other folds over his right arm, like a man holding a large baby in an elaborate christening gown. In his left hand, he held the slender rope. Again and again he threw the net, badly at first, but then with mounting grace, until it actually did look like a wedding dress, billowing open in the moonlight onto the grass.

As we watched him gather and throw, gather and throw, I could almost hear the splash of the weights hitting the ocean waves, almost smell the salt tang of the sea air, almost hear the pitty-pat the mullet would make on the wet sand when he dumped them from the net. I thought how good they would taste when Mama fried them in corn meal and Crisco. My mouth watered, and I itched to go fishing.

I didn't know the tide was already turning.

Two

The rule was: church before fishing. The next day was Palm Sunday, and our family went to what turned out to be our last service before everything changed.

On the way out the church door after the service, Daddy shook Brother Warren Dimmesdale's hand and thanked him for giving us all something to think about. It's what Daddy told the preacher every Sunday, and I couldn't ever tell if it meant he agreed with the subject of the sermon or not. Mama apologized to Brother Dimmesdale because we weren't going to make it back for Training Union and Evening Worship.

We were going to the beach, to try out Daddy's new mullet net!

I wasn't sorry at all, and in fact had to work hard to keep from skipping on my way to our pea-soup-colored Rambler station wagon, which we'd nicknamed the Green Hornet. We raced home, changed into our swimsuits, ate peanut butter-and-banana sandwiches, and then hit the road.

During the drive to Atlantic Beach, Daddy dreamed out loud about making a shrimp net, too, to use for night casting at the public docks on the St. Johns River. He said he'd use a big white spotlight and clay shrimp-meal balls to attract the shrimp. I finished reading *Peter Pan* on the way, and soon we parked at a lot beside the ocean.

"Honey-bunny, come carry this for me, please," Daddy called out from behind the station wagon. I walked around the open tailgate where he draped the mullet net across my shoulder.

I wrapped the pull-line around my hand and felt the slap-slap of the silver weights at the bottom of the net against my legs as I walked toward the scooped-out crossover section of the dunes.

Our family always gravitated to water and the natural pull of the tides. Daddy worked hard at his day job, making price signs at the Winn-Dixie print shop to support us, but he worked religiously in his off-hours on fishing, for the pure love of it. He fished with a rod and reel from Jacksonville's low bridges, with a bait bucket by his side and cars whizzing past his rear end. He also fished in the Bass River with a cane pole from a little aluminum rowboat Mama had bought him from the Pic N' Save one Christmas.

Mama loved being near the water, too, but she had a harder time relaxing. Daddy said it was because she was afraid that if she sat still too long, her past would catch up with her. She'd had a rough childhood, and then a good bit of the raising of her younger brother fell on Mama after their mother died. I never knew my real grandma, and Paw Paw was old by the time I knew him, but getting away from him was one reason Mama married Daddy when she was only sixteen.

Mama created a safe, spotless home for Daddy, Jimmy, and me, and could be tons of fun, unless something happened to disturb her carefully-ordered world. That something might be as innocent as my brother or me not doing our chores fast enough to suit her, or Daddy looking just a little too long at a pretty woman walking by. Then the monster hiding inside her would come out, screaming, yelling, and hitting. I spent most of my time with Mama trying to make sure that nobody inside or outside the family riled her. The Bible said *Blessed are the peacemakers,* and I liked things peaceful.

"Jimmy, come get this ice chest," shouted Mama to my brother, who was already walking toward the beach, flip-flops flapping against his heels and beach towel slung around his neck. Somehow, when Daddy asked you to do something, it sounded like a pleasant request; Mama always barked orders. Jimmy turned and went back to the car, scowling. Sometimes, when she ordered him around and her back was to him, he'd give her the *Heil Hitler* salute—but never while she was watching.

"Would it break your jaw to say *please?*" Daddy muttered.

I led the way to the beach as Jimmy followed with our silver cooler, his biceps bulging. Daddy trooped behind, somehow carrying a shovel, the mop bucket, two beach blankets, and a sack of charcoal. I don't know how he didn't drop something. Mama brought up the rear, toting two paper grocery sacks that, I knew from prior trips, held suntan lotion, lighter fluid, beach toys, food and RC colas.

We walked single file, far down the beach, past the other families with their picnics, the teenagers slathered in baby oil lying on blankets, and the surfers with their M&M-colored boards. As we passed the pretty girls, I walked backward and watched my brother's head swivel like a wind-vane in a stiff breeze, and I watched Mama watch Daddy.

Jimmy started singing a popular song from the radio: *I'm a girl watcher watching girls go by* …. Daddy chimed in with *My, my, my*, at the right time. But it was the wrong time, because we were passing a blonde-haired lady in a red-striped bikini, and Mama snarled, "Take a picture, it'll last longer." Daddy rolled his eyes and winked at me as if he didn't care, but after that he marched with his head down, looking only at the sand in front of him.

I wished there were no other ladies on the beach, at least not pretty ones, so Mama's lips wouldn't be all pinched and Daddy wouldn't look like a dog that'd been swatted with the newspaper.

We stopped when we reached our favorite spot, a comfortable distance past everyone else. Vine-covered dunes made a little wind-break, and a broad expanse of soft white sand stretched almost to the water's edge, where broken shells littered the hard-packed gray sand. We had figured out, without saying it aloud, that the farther we stayed from the bathing beauties, the less likely Mama would be to stay jealous and angry. Mama busied herself setting up a little camp of blankets held down by the rest of our gear, slamming things around a little harder than need be, working off her snit.

Daddy sent me running ahead to scout for schools of mullet as they swam toward us, parallel to the shore. He was most likely getting me out from underfoot, but I felt useful.

The water was choppy, and I had to concentrate hard to see the brownish-gray, fast-moving schools. When I saw them, I gave a war whoop and pointed. Daddy waded out, up to his waist. As the school swept past, he cast the net at just the right moment, then hauled it to shore, full of flopping, wriggling mullet. In just a few casts we had more than the four of us could hope to eat.

I ran to Daddy with our big white mop bucket, and he tossed the fish inside, after picking each one up by the tail and dipping it delicately into the ocean. I felt sorry for the poor mullet, who thought they were free and tried to swim away, only to find themselves bumping against the walls of the bucket after the sand was washed off.

"Well done, Chief Catch-um Heap Big Fish," I told him.

"Well done, Eagle-Eye Tiger-Lily."

While I had his attention, and he seemed happy over catching so many fish in his new net, I thought I'd ask Daddy an important question.

"Daddy, don't you think Mama's beautiful? And she's pretty nice, too, when she's not mad."

"Your mama's got nothing to worry about. A man don't go out for hamburger when he's got steak at home." The second part of his answer didn't make any sense to me at the time, but the first part, about not worrying, made me happy.

Farther up on shore, where the sand was always dry and the tide had no chance of dousing our cook fire, Mama had dug a shallow pit with the shovel, lined it with charcoal, and thrown tinfoil-covered roasting ears of corn and fat Vidalias (the sweetest onions known to mankind) onto the white-hot coals. Daddy called Jimmy back from his girl-watching and perpetual pursuit of the perfect shark's tooth among the shells on the shore. They headed, gutted, and scaled the fish, throwing the scraps to the screeching gulls.

While they worked, I confided in Mama. "Daddy told me you're the prettiest, nicest lady he knows, and not to worry about a thing, 'cause he likes steak better than hamburgers." I wrinkled my nose. "But, I thought we were having fish."

Mama laughed and waved Daddy and Jimmy over. "We are, Baby; we are." Her face looked pretty when she laughed. Only her eyes still looked a tiny bit sad.

We cooked the fish in a wire basket over the coals. To me, the best part of supper was the onions. We pulled them, soot-black from the fire, and slowly peeled away the burned outer layers, scorching our fingers, enticed by the heavenly aroma. Inside, the tender middles were succulent and perfect, sweet as candy. In all my years, I've never tasted any meal so fine as that one of ocean-fresh mullet with hot buttered corn and Vidalias, in the sand on that beach, by the campfire with my family.

After supper, Jimmy reclined on his beach towel, rubbing his belly. He belched. We all laughed. Daddy belched louder, and we laughed again. Daddy and Mama cuddled on the old blanket. He whispered something to her, and she giggled. I sat in the sand by the fire, my sunburned legs crossed like a proper TV Indian's, and felt the warm air cool down one degree at a time. Daddy blew Woody Guthrie train songs on his harmonica as the sun sank behind the dunes and the sea fell asleep in front of us.

I prayed life would always stay exactly like this.

Three

Always didn't last a week, because Mama wasn't the only one in our family with a jealous bone. The following Saturday, the day before Easter Sunday, I got mad enough to cuss. But only under my breath, where Mama couldn't hear.

We were at the Baptist Home for Children to take our cousins, the three Harper girls, out to eat at Morrison's Cafeteria. Suzannah, that big baby, was going to ride between Mama and Daddy in the front seat of the Green Hornet. Delilah jumped in the back seat next to Jimmy and started making googly eyes at him. Priscilla joined them.

"Hop in the way-back, Honey," Mama ordered, pulling her car door shut.

I strangled a whimper of protest from outside her door and appealed to Daddy with a roll of my eyes, but he just cranked the car and tapped the steering wheel, ready to get going toward a plateful of butter beans, country ham, and collard greens.

I crawled past the tailgate and settled onto a thin camping mattress Daddy had thrown back there for Doodle the Poodle. If my black, curly-haired dog hadn't licked my face just then with his rough tongue, I might have cried with frustration. At ten, I felt practically grown, but because my cousins were our *company* for lunch, they got to ride in the regular seats with Mama, Daddy, and Jimmy, while I was stuffed in the way-back with the dog. Our silver ice chest, there to keep our cousins' surprise Easter basket candy from melting, made it even more crowded. I couldn't even stretch out my legs all the way.

"Roll down the window back there, Honey-bunny, get some fresh air blowing through this barge," Daddy said. He added a wink in the rearview mirror that I'm sure was supposed to make me feel better.

On another day, I might have begged to ride way in the back, but that day I felt left-out and less-than. I cranked the window down, with my bottom lip stuck out as far as it would go.

The Harper girls were the next best thing to orphans, but you wouldn't guess it by the way they talked about their parents. Their daddy was my mama's younger brother Travis, but he and the girls' mama, Aunt Rita Faye, either couldn't, or wouldn't, take care of their kids (depending on who you asked). On the ride to Morrison's, while they caught Mama and Daddy up on their mama's health and their daddy's whereabouts, I put down *Tom Sawyer* and stared out the car window, silently reviewing the gossip I'd gleaned about them up to that point, by listening to Mama and her step sisters over the years.

Uncle Travis was an on-again, off-again drunkard, and Aunt Rita Faye was schizophrenic. That part wasn't gossip; that was her official diagnosis, and she'd spent years up at Chattahootchee, in the state mental hospital, to prove it. Shock therapy was how they treated what ailed Aunt Rita Faye in those days. I felt sorry for her, because even the name of that treatment sounded awful. We didn't mention our aunt and uncle much to outsiders.

In between their fights, and Aunt Rita Faye's visits to the loony bin, these two sad, messed-up people had managed to spawn four children. Their oldest was Delilah, born when Travis only drank at parties and Rita Faye was just about the prettiest woman in town. Delilah was quickly followed by Priscilla. Uncle Travis started drinking every night of the week, and Aunt Rita Faye's hips weren't so slim any more. Little Travis came along next, and while Travis Sr. nearly busted a gut with pride over his fine, fat baby boy, Rita Faye had a hard time juggling three children, two of them still in diapers. By the time Suzannah came along, Uncle Travis drank all day, every day, and forgot to notice that little Suzie had her mama's unforgettable black eyes.

One by one, Uncle Travis and Aunt Rita Faye let their daughters slip away. Before any of them turned ten, Delilah, Priscilla, and Suzannah were all sent to the Baptist Home.

We'd visit the girls on birthdays and holidays, with baskets and gifts, and sometimes we'd go for no reason at all, except that they were family and they needed us. To Jimmy and me, they didn't have it so bad. There was a big swimming pool (a great advantage, it seemed to us, since our house wasn't air-conditioned.) There were ball fields and basketball courts, and even horses to ride. Sometimes, when Mama would whip me with a belt or a switch for no good reason, I'd think it sure would be nice if she'd let me go live at the Baptist Home. I loved horses, at least the ones in books, and Mama sure could whip hard. She never stopped once you got the point, either. She whipped until she got tired of whipping.

That particular Saturday, while the cafeteria lady in her white apron spooned banana pudding into little bowls and set them on our trays, I decided to see if I couldn't outsmart Suzie into giving up the front seat on the ride back. "Y'all got any dogs at the Home, Suzie?" I asked.

She shook her head and inched her tray forward along the rails, in the line just in front of me.

"That's too bad," I said, dripping sympathy. "There ain't nothing as sweet as a cute little dog like Doodle."

"He sure is cute," she agreed.

"Too bad Mama won't let him sit with you up there in the front seat," I said. "If you rode in the way-back, you could scratch him behind the ears. That gets his hind leg going like crazy."

Suzie laughed. "Aw!"

I leaned closer to her, a big grin on my face. "He likes to lay on his back on that mattress and get his belly rubbed. You should see him wiggle!"

Her eyes shined. "Can I ride back there with y'all?"

"There ain't enough room for two," I said, "and you might get dog-hair on your clothes."

"I don't care about no dog hair," Suzie said.

"He doesn't know you. He might get scared."

"You could introduce us, before we get going."

"I reckon I could do that," I agreed.

"Do what?" Mama said from up the line, where she was counting heads and Daddy was paying the man at the cash register.

Suzie beamed. "Honey's gonna let me ride in the way-back with Doodle!"

Mama frowned. "I ain't taking you back to the Home with your good clothes smelling like a dog," she said to Suzie. "You can play with Doodle the next time you come to our house for a visit."

Then her hard stare fell on me. "And she ain't gonna whitewash your fence for you, neither."

I'd forgotten who gave me that book to read in the first place.

When Mama made up her mind, it stayed made up, so I settled for accidentally bumping my tray into Suzie's, sloshing her chocolate milk on her fried chicken and into her mountain of black-eyed peas.

After lunch, Daddy pulled the Green Hornet up next to the shady front porch that spanned the length of the red brick Baptist Home and unloaded the cooler. We sat in a row of big white rocking chairs, sipping iced tea while the girls tore into their Easter baskets, cooing over the candy and stuffed bunnies. Suzannah slipped over to where Mama sat rocking and eased into her lap. Mama rocked my nine-year-old cousin like a little baby, and I got that icky feeling in the pit of my stomach, like I did sometimes when Daddy watched Shirley Temple movies on TV and made me jealous, talking about how cute and talented she was.

"I hope you like your Easter candy. We don't keep sweets in the house, since Daddy's diabetic," Jimmy hinted, so Delilah offered him a foil-covered chocolate Easter egg from the basket we'd brought her.

"No sweets?" she said. "That must be awful." Priscilla held her basket out to me, and I took one, still feeling crabby, although I also felt lucky, like I did every time anybody mentioned diabetes. I'd watched Daddy give himself insulin shots in the arm, thigh, and hip, but the thing that always gave me the heebie-jeebies was when he pinched a fold of his stomach and jabbed the just-boiled syringe in with the little silver "gun." Plus, when he went to the bathroom, he had to check the sugar level in his urine by wetting on a little test stick. Yuck.

Mama told me once that Jimmy and I both had a fifty-fifty chance of getting the disease, but so far we'd flipped heads, where Daddy'd flipped tails. Mama only rarely let us have candy, though. She said it wasn't fair to Daddy. This time when I glanced at her, she gave a quick nod. An Easter miracle. I gobbled the chocolate egg as quick as I could peel the foil off, before she could change her mind. Daddy didn't seem to notice.

"Have you heard from my brother lately?" Mama asked Priscilla.

"Yes, ma'am, Aunt Rose," she answered. "Daddy called just last weekend. He said he's getting a good new job, managing a convenience store, and pretty soon he's gonna bring Mama home from the hospital."

Delilah's eyes shone. "Then he's gonna buy us a nice big house, with an upstairs and a downstairs," she said.

Priscilla piped up. "We told him we want bunk beds, one for each of us."

"And a puppy," said Suzannah, sitting up, and then burying her head back in Mama's shoulder.

"One for each of you?" Daddy teased. I imagined three puppies getting all tangled up under the feet of three girls, making a huge mess and a bigger ruckus. That's all Aunt Rita Faye needed. She'd be back in the booby hatch in no time.

Mama pasted a big old plastic smile on her face and agreed with all of them that *yes*, their daddy would have a good job soon, and *yes*, their mama would be feeling better soon, and *yes*, they would sure enough all be living together again before they knew it, in a big nice house with stairs and bunk beds for all the children.

I shook my head in disgust, out of Mama's line of sight. *Sure they would.*

After the girls kissed and hugged us good-bye, I climbed into the backseat beside Jimmy for the ride to our grandparents' combination house and store. Doodle stood up on his hind legs with his front paws on the seat back, so I could scratch his head while we rode along. I was still mad about the way Mama'd cuddled Suzannah, so I lit into her as best as I could from the backseat of the car, without making her mad enough to turn around and slap my mouth. She could slap you into the middle of next week.

"Why do you do it, Mama? Why do you tell them that no-good daddy of theirs is going to come get them, when you know he won't quit drinking?"

"Everybody needs a little hope in their life, Honey. And we'll keep praying for Uncle Travis and Aunt Rita Faye, like always."

I sat there thinking, *I'm praying he'll choke on his beer and go straight to H-E-double-L, and I hope old crazy Aunt Rita Faye gets one of those shock treatments so strong it makes her hair curly and knocks some sense into her so she'll come and get her daughters.*

What made me the maddest was that Uncle Travis and Aunt Rita Faye had managed to keep Little Travis. At that age, I hated my aunt and uncle for demonstrating their belief that boys were worthy and girls were worthless.

When Little Travis started school, the social workers had come sniffing around. To keep his son, Uncle Travis had to sober up a little and show up at work on time for a while.

He had to check Aunt Rita Faye out of the hospital and pay the rent that month. Then he went to court and made sure he kept his precious boy.

Now I know that did not make Little Travis the lucky one.

I remembered how mean I'd felt toward the girls all day, how I hadn't been a very good Christian, trying to trick little Suzie and all.

Up in the front seat, Mama fretted about her nieces. "I can hardly stand to leave them there like that," she said. Mama collected stray people like some women collected cats or buttons or dolls. Mean as she could sometimes be, she loved taking care of others.

Daddy reached across the seat and patted her hand. "Call your sisters together when we get to your folks', Rose." He glanced into the backseat, where he noticed me and Jimmy listening. "To discuss ... what we discussed ... discussing."

Four

In those years, my Paw Paw owned a bait-and-tackle store on the shore of Bass River, up the road from our house, near the bridge. I wanted him to change its name to The Old Man and the Sea, after my daddy's favorite book by Ernest Hemingway, but Paw Paw called it Harper's Bait and Tackle, because he lacked imagination. The store sold ice and snacks, but the huge sign across the front of the store screamed *Beer-Bait-Cigarettes!!!*

Even without the sign, or if you couldn't read, you would have known what was sold there by its smell, which embarrassed me, especially the times we brought any of my friends along. In the front of the store were the two big bait tanks: one held live shrimp, the other shiners. I liked watching them swim in a huge tangle, but felt sorry for them. I wondered if they knew they were going to become some big fish's dinner, if they were scared. It reminded me of the way I felt when I went to Katy Barrington's house to play. Nicknamed Kat, she was the only other girl who lived within walking distance of our house. But even though she was a year younger than me, she was lots bigger, and I usually came home with a black eye, a busted lip, or at least some wounded pride. I avoided her if I could help it.

At Harper's Bait and Tackle you could also get dead shrimp on ice from the freezer, or fat, ugly nightcrawlers from the worm-bed out back. There were two rusty old shovels stuck in the dirt out there, for turning up the worms. Paw Paw claimed he could grunt them to the top, but, although I begged, I never saw him do it. Some folks liked to fish with the hideous red, yellow, and black crickets, big as my hand, that Paw Paw kept in a wooden box with a screened lid. They gave me the willies.

The aromas of the other two hot commodities, beer and cigarettes, surrounded Paw Paw Harper like a cloud. I held my breath while I hugged him hello. Mama was always afraid the beer would kill him, if the cigarettes didn't get him first.

Maw Maw didn't smell like much of anything at all, next to Paw Paw. She wore no perfume or makeup, dressed like a man in a work shirt and dungarees, and cussed worse than any three sailors. Daddy said she was a no-nonsense gal. Her language made Mama get all pinch-lipped, but it was Maw Maw I secretly imitated when I was mad. Still do.

Maw Maw kissed me on top of the head, holding a Virginia Slims cigarette of her own high up in the air so it wouldn't burn me. "Hey, Stink-bait," she said. It seemed like everybody had a different nickname for me, but hers was my favorite, because it wasn't just a mash-up of my real name. She'd simply named me that the first time she'd changed my dirty diaper.

There were three hard and fast rules laid down by Mama and Daddy when we visited Maw Maw and Paw Paw at the store.

Rule Number One: Don't ask for anything from the shelves. We had to wait until it was offered. Jimmy made straight for the rack of comic books, like always. Me, I was mesmerized by the little Barbie doll knockoffs in plastic bikinis. I liked to play with them in the sand parking lot, and then dunk them in the shiner tank, pretending it was the Amazon, and the fish were piranhas.

But that day a pair of jewel-colored plastic high heeled shoes caught my eye. Jimmy and I stood in front of the shelves with our hands tightly clasped behind our backs, since Mama always told us, "Look with your eyes, not with your hands." We lingered there, pining away in front of the treasures, all big eyes and sweet expressions, until Paw Paw broke down and called out, "Take what y'all want, now." Jimmy grabbed his comic while I snatched up the high heels. Maw Maw handed me a Yoo-hoo and Jimmy a Co-Cola from the cooler, popping off the caps with the bottle opener built into the side of the case.

"Thank you," we called out, as we barreled back onto the front porch of the store. Jimmy settled on the wooden steps with Superman. I kicked off my flip-flops and changed into Cinderella's slippers.

Rule Number Two: Don't play the *Lotta Smokes* or *Hobo Bill* punchboards, even if you'd saved a quarter or two from your allowance. Maw Maw and Paw Paw sold chances to hard-looking fishermen who punched out their numbers with a metal stylus tied to the counter with a long string. If they picked the lucky numbers, Paw Paw paid them from the cash drawer. They cussed and carried on if their numbers didn't win. I don't remember ever actually seeing anybody win, but that was okay because punchboards were gambling, and for us Southern Baptists, that was a sin. Actually, it seemed like 'most everything that Harper's Bait and Tackle sold was a sin, except the bait. And most of that was ugly as sin, after all, especially those crickets.

Rule Number Three: Never, ever, under any circumstances, get in a car with Paw Paw driving. No matter what.

"Why can't we ever ride in Paw Paw's car?" I asked Jimmy. The plastic shoes made a satisfying clomp, clomp, clomp as I sashayed across the clapboard porch, pretending I was in the Miss America pageant.

He looked up from his comic book. "Paw Paw drives too fast when he's drinking, and he's always drinking. Don't mention it—that would be rude. Just don't get in the car."

One by one, our mama's two step-sisters arrived, summoned on the telephone in the store for the mysterious "discussion." Our tribe was connected via party line, so staying in touch was a simple matter, and we knew who was calling before we picked up the phone, by each relative's special ring. At nine o'clock, 'most every night of our lives, Mama, the aunts, and Maw Maw said their good-night, sleep-tights over the line before snapping off their bedside lamps.

I clomped over to give Aunt Bonnie and Aunt Violet hugs, turning inside out with curiosity, but Jimmy wouldn't let me go back into the store.

He even let me read his Superman comic when he was finished with it, while he moseyed around back. My brother and Jimmy Olsen, Superman's photographer sidekick, had the same first name, which I thought was an omen. Writing stories and taking pictures for a newspaper would be the two coolest jobs in the world.

Jimmy's real-life hero was Rocco Morabito, a news photographer from the Jacksonville Journal who'd won a big prize for a picture he took of two linemen working on a power pole. One of the men was hanging upside down, unconscious, while the other was blowing air into him using something called mouth-to-mouth. I'd giggled when I'd first seen the picture Jimmy cut from the newspaper and hung on the wall of his bedroom, because it looked like two men kissing and I didn't understand it. But after Jimmy explained what was happening, it wasn't funny anymore; it seemed heroic. The lineman who'd been electrocuted woke up and got better. The photo was called *The Kiss of Life*.

If it got any hotter on the front porch of the store, I was gonna stop breathing myself. I sipped my Yoo-hoo and wondered what was going on with the grown-ups inside the store.

Finished with Superman, and already bored with my new high heels, I peeked in the front left window, where I could see, but not hear, the women talking. I moved to the window on the right front, closer to the cash register where they were gathered. When I saw Maw Maw glance out the store's window, I ducked down into a crouch under the sill. I slid down to my bottom and sat with my legs straight out, so I wouldn't spill my Yoo-hoo.

Maw Maw was Mama's stepmother. The details were murky surrounding the accident that killed Mama's real mother, but I'd learned what little I knew on the subject by being very quiet and listening to my mama speculate with Daddy about it over the years.

Paw Paw and my real grandmother had lived near the Jacksonville Coliseum, close to downtown. On the night my grandmother died, a man could still attend a sporting event at the Coliseum and walk home with his wife in safety.

I scratched at a mosquito bite on my arm and listened as hard as I could, straining to hear the women through the window pane without being seen. Their voices were a pleasant, indistinct murmur.

In the South, certain things are never said outright—even a child knows that. They are hinted at, danced around, and mulled over, until, finally, if you're bright and pay close enough attention, after years of hearing bits and pieces of stories and adding two and two to make five, you get the gist.

No one ever said directly, within my hearing, that Paw Paw had been drinking all day before that game at the Coliseum, and no one accused him of having a few more pulls from his hip-flask at the game itself. No one ever told me outright that my grandmother and Paw Paw were having an ugly argument about another woman on that walk home. The story was simply that they weren't getting along very well in their last years together. But Mama hinted that he'd sure married Maw Maw awful quick after the funeral. No one ever, ever said that Paw Paw pushed my real grandmother into the path of a speeding car in a drunken rage that night, but the details slowly came together until one night the image appeared in a dream that sent me bolt upright in the bed, sweating and screaming and crying for a grandmother who died years before I was born. Maybe it was only a dream. Maybe I blamed Paw Paw wrongly. But I did wonder. And I kept my distance, just in case.

The night Grandma died, my mama, fourteen at the time, was left in charge of Travis, who was two years younger than she was. My mother was a mama's girl, and was so scared of Paw Paw at the time that he could make her wet herself by pointing a finger at her in anger. He'd broken her nose with his fist the year before, when she stepped between him and her mama during one of their fights.

Mama told me she doesn't remember anything about her mother's funeral, or even getting the news of her death. She does remember opening the door and seeing the preacher standing there with her daddy. She remembers that clearly, over and over and over, opening that door, and seeing them standing there together, hats in hand—"We've got some bad news, Rosie"—then a dark void.

Tears welled up in my eyes, thinking how scared and sad she must have felt. Sometimes, when Mama acted mean, I thought about that sad, motherless girl, and didn't get mad back.

I took a couple of big gulps of my Yoo-hoo and felt a little better.

Mama said she sleepwalked through her mother's funeral and the weeks following. She got up every day, washed herself, got dressed, ate the food put before her, and did what she was told to do. She spoke not a word to anyone. Mama said she woke up two months later. They told her she'd had "brain fever," and she didn't seem to remember anything at all about the time that had gone by.

When she came back to herself, her mother was gone, Paw Paw had a new wife, and Mama had two new step sisters.

I wondered if maybe that was why Mama didn't trust men, and tried to keep our world so safe and small. She always kept such a watchful eye on Daddy. I wanted to tell her Daddy was different than Paw Paw, that he loved her and me and Jimmy more than anything, that she had nothing to worry about. I wanted to let her know that Daddy would never hurt us or leave us. But I didn't know how to bring it up. And I didn't know then that I was wrong, at least about the leaving.

Aunt Bonnie raised her voice. My ears pricked up; she sounded angry. "Rita Faye ain't as crazy as she lets on," she said. "She gets a nice rest every time she checks into Chattahootchee."

Aunt Violet snorted. "She gets tired of wiping little butts and noses, and then takes herself a little vacation."

"Y'all are just as mean as snakes," Maw Maw shushed her daughters.

"I don't think shock treatments qualify as a vacation," Mama said. "I hear they make you sit in a tub of ice, then run electricity through it." To my cold-natured Mama, that would be the very description of Hades.

"Bless her heart," Aunt Bonnie and Aunt Violet said, right at the same time, as if that made it okay.

The sun blazed, and my Yoo-hoo was all gone. I was glad the ladies were finally talking loud enough for me to hear, but just then Jimmy rounded the corner of the store and plopped down on the step. He crooked his finger at me, so I crawled over to sit beside him, hoping he wouldn't tell on me for listening to the grownups. He bumped my shoulder with his, and tickled the back of my neck, just above my collar. "Didja like the Superman story, Lil' Bit?" he asked, grinning, as I handed him back his comic book. He liked calling me that, after Bit-O-Honey candy bars.

"Yep," I started to say, but then the tickle I'd thought was my brother's fingers on my neck skittered down my backbone, throwing me into a panic when I suddenly remembered he'd been out behind the store, and what Paw Paw kept out there. Crickets! Down the back of my shirt! A primal whoop erupted from my throat, and I did a war dance that would have made Tiger Lily proud, tearing the bottom of my blouse out of my shorts, shaking and contorting, shrieking, "Get it out! GETITOUT!!!" while Jimmy roared and rocked so hard with laughter that he rolled off the steps onto the sand parking lot. The cricket fell from the bottom of my shirt into the sand and lay stunned at my feet as Mama, Daddy, Maw Maw, Paw Paw, Aunt Bonnie and Aunt Violet poured onto the front porch to see who was being murdered. I jumped on my brother and started pounding. He just laughed harder.

"Damn kids," Maw Maw muttered. "You sure you can handle another one?" she asked Mama.

"What did she say?" I asked, as Daddy pulled me off Jimmy, locking my scrawny, flailing arms behind my back. *Was Mama expecting a baby?*

Daddy eased up on my arms and explained to Jimmy and me. "Paw Paw and Maw Maw have given Travis and Rita Faye a few years to straighten up and get their kids back. They've finally realized that isn't likely to happen."

Maw Maw spoke up. "We aren't going to watch our grandkids grow up in an orphanage, so the three girls are being parceled out among the relatives."

"We didn't want to leave any of the girls behind at the Home, so all the aunts had to agree," said Paw Paw.

"Priscilla will live with me," said Aunt Bonnie.

"I'm taking Delilah," Aunt Violet said.

"We'll get Suzannah," said Mama. Of course. Mama's new baby.

I went cold and still inside at that news. Everyone stared at me.

"Where will she sleep?" I asked, squinting against the sun's glare.

"She'll share your room," Mama said. "The two of you can sleep in your double bed, and Maw Maw's giving us another chest of drawers to squeeze in under the window. It'll be like a never-ending slumber party." She watched me, full of hope and big plans. *Let me do this*, her blue eyes begged. *Don't make trouble. Be happy about it.*

I wasn't used to being asked what I thought. I kind of liked it.

"Will she eat our food?" I wanted to know.

Daddy grinned. "She's a little bitty gal, and there's plenty of food. Don't worry."

I kicked the sand with the toe of my Ked, and bit my lip to keep from sassing my parents. Great. I had a hateful big brother, and I wouldn't even be the baby of the family anymore.

Four is the perfect number for a family—one boy, one girl, and two parents, I thought, as Daddy sped the Green Hornet back across town from Harper's Bait and Tackle, leading a caravan that included my grandparents and aunts, toward the Baptist Home for Children to check our cousins out for extended "visits." All sorts of legal mumbo-jumbo still had to be taken care of, Mama explained. Even the girls' absent parents had to give written consent to the new living arrangements, which confused me— hadn't they given their kids away? But there was no time like the present to get the ball rolling. No one had ever accused Mama of being a patient person, and no one ever would.

I reached over the back seat and gave Doodle a scratch behind his ears. He licked my hand, and then plopped down on his mattress for a nap. I thought of Jesus finding all of his disciples asleep on the ground on the worst night of HIS life. "Could you not wait with me an hour?" he had asked them.

Would my sleepy little dog, at least, still love me best?

Five

Once their minds had been made up to provide loving homes for their nieces, Mama and the aunts did not let the sun set on their plans. What better morning for my cousins to wake up to their new lives than Easter Sunday? The Harper girls greeted the news wide-eyed that Saturday night, with excited chatter and hugs all around, then shed a few quiet tears as they realized that at the same time they gained new homes, they'd be parted from each other. Their tears over leaving their sisters made my concerns feel petty, and kept me quiet on the ride home.

When we arrived at our house, Mama and Suzannah chirped like happy birds, unpacking the brown Winn-Dixie grocery sacks that held Suzie's clothes, books, and toys into my drawers, closets, and shelves where I hastily made room for them. We'd have more space once Paw Paw delivered the extra chest of drawers Maw Maw was donating.

After we settled into my double bed, much later than my usual eight o'clock bedtime, I told Suzie good night and then turned on my side, with my back to her. I stared at the wall for a long time, then closed my eyes for what felt like just a few minutes before I heard Mama hollering for us to *rise 'n' shine*. Breakfast was ready.

In those days, Sunday was usually my favorite day of the week. Our family always woke up early on the Lord's Day to enjoy a big country breakfast together, and then, spit-shined and well-fed, we'd lope down Ridge Road the half mile to Beverly Hills Baptist Church. Daddy was quite a talented artist and had donated his time to paint the beautiful black lettering on the big white sign outside the sanctuary. I liked to stop and admire the straight-as-an-arrow way the letters advertised the times for classes and services on our way into the building.

But this Easter Sunday morning, I didn't wake up alone, and furthermore, Mama told Suzie she was welcome to try on some church dresses I had that were getting a little too tight. That almost took the starch right out of my new Easter dress.

Once we were at Sunday school, our teacher, Mrs. Nemeth, had me introduce my cousin, and then passed around a small glass bottle she fished from the bottom of her huge, cluttered purse. "What do you think these are, girls?" she asked me and the other third- and fourth-graders as we peered at the tiny black balls in the jar. Pills? Bugs? Pepper? None of us, not even Lil' Orphan Suz-Annie, knew the right answer.

"The Bible tells us we only need faith the size of one of these little mustard seeds to move a mountain," she explained. "Just imagine."

I closed my eyes and imagined God moving a tall, mountain-sized jar of yellow mustard in between our house and the Baptist Home for Children, but when I opened them, Suzie still sat beside me in a folding chair, wearing my Easter dress from last year, black patent leather shoes, and frilly white socks.

She was one of the most beautiful girls I'd ever seen, the spitting image of Aunt Rita Faye in a black and white photo Mama had, taken in their late teens. Rita Faye was wearing a stunning white bandeau bathing suit against luscious tanned skin, her black hair blowing in the sea-breeze, black eyes flashing in the sun. My boyish blonde pixie haircut emphasized how plain I looked, even in brand-spanking-new Easter finery, compared to Suzannah with her flowing locks.

After Sunday school, I walked with Suzie to the sanctuary, conscious of the friendly stares and whispers her presence caused.

Beverly Hills Baptist Church was housed in a plain, two-story, white cement-block structure with a modest steeple and only a single step leading to its double-wide front doors. But appearances were deceiving. It was a thriving little church in the Southern Baptist Convention, serving a congregation of two hundred souls, give or take. On the Lord's Day, there was Sunday school, Morning Worship Service, home for dinner and a short rest (which I usually spent in our hammock with a book) then back for Training Union and Evening Worship.

On Wednesdays, before Prayer Meeting, boys went to RAs, which stood for Royal Ambassadors, while girls my age went to GAs, which stood for Girls in Action. Older girls had Acteens. These classes taught us about missionaries, and we lived in awe of Annie Armstrong and Lottie Moon. I personally dreamed of harvesting souls for Jesus on the distant shores of China or Africa, like they had—or maybe fighting evil with prayer and forgiveness, like Corrie Ten Boom in *The Hiding Place*.

I wondered if any of those missionaries had enough faith to work miracles. That would sure come in handy.

Our church was well-known for dinners-on-the-grounds, which were held for almost any imaginable occasion. Beverly Hills was heavy with outstanding Southern cooks who liked to try to outdo each other's fried chicken, green bean or sweet-potato casseroles, fruit pies, cakes of all descriptions, and biscuits big as dinner plates, smothered in sausage gravy.

We also had a sizable choir, led by Brother Sweeney, who couldn't carry a tune in a bucket but made up for his lack of talent with volume and enthusiasm. Once in a while, some grumbler would suggest replacing Brother Sweeney with a choir director who could actually sing, and our preacher, Brother Dimmesdale, would cheerfully agree that the grumbler was welcome to inform Brother Sweeney of that decision. A brave few made the attempt, but Brother Sweeney always gave such a smiling, inspired rebuttal about making a joyful noise unto the Lord that the grumblers never quite got the job done.

When we wore the covers off our Baptist Hymnals, the Ladies Sewing Guild, led by my mama, simply re-covered them and we kept right on singing.

In spite of all the good food and loud music, the main draw for the big crowds that packed the pews service after service was Warren Dimmesdale himself. Hollywood handsome, he could preach the ears off a cornfield. And sing? He'd do a rendition of "He Touched Me" that made the hairs on your arms and the back of your neck rise up and shout, "Hallelujah!"

"Genesis, Exodus, Leviticus, Numbers …" I chanted under my breath on my way into the sanctuary after Sunday school. I had to stay sharp to keep winning the Training Union Bible drills. That was my secret weapon; I'd memorized all the books of the Bible, Old and New Testaments, so while the other kids fumbled around, looking for Deuteronomy or Second Samuel, I'd be on my feet, whiz-bang, already reading aloud the verse the teacher called out. The other kids might not like me winning all the time, but Mama sure looked proud every time I handed her another satin Bible Drill Champion ribbon. Her Bible was stuffed so full of them it would hardly close. I was a little worried, that Easter Sunday morning, now that Suzie was living with us. I knew the kids at the Baptist Home were required to attend church every week. I wondered whether they ever held Bible drills, and how quick on the draw my littlest cousin might be. I'd have to watch out.

Our family sat in a favorite pew on the left-hand side of the church, third row back, with me closest to the center aisle. Jimmy always sat in the middle of the pew, next to Mama, who sat by Daddy, who sat next to me so he could grab the back of my neck with his right hand if I got too fidgety. That was his quiet signal for me to settle down, and it worked real well, because if I didn't get still right away, his grip grew tighter and tighter until it actually hurt. I didn't like that one little bit.

That day, Suzie squeezed into the pew between Mama and Daddy. I figured Mama would scoot her along, since she liked to share her hymnal with Daddy, but the little brat got away with it. Must have been because it was her first time, I thought.

It wasn't actually fair that they got us all riled up singing songs about Saints marching in and onward Christian soldiers, then expected us to sit still like little church mice instead of wiggling and tapping our feet. War seemed to be on Brother Dimmesdale's mind all the time, anyway, never mind that he sang *Peace in the Valley* pretty enough to make the angels cry just before the offertory hymn.

He mentioned he'd be preaching from the Beatitudes on this beautiful Resurrection Sunday, and *bam*, the Bible drill queen turned to Matthew 5 before he even cited the passage. I showed my open Bible to Daddy, who nudged Mama, who gave me a proud wink. I sat up a little straighter.

"… Blessed are the peacemakers, for they shall be called the children of God," intoned the preacher. I'll bet God sounds just like that, I thought. Of course, Brother Dimmesdale could read my math book aloud and it would sound wonderful. I would have watched him brush his teeth for an hour on Sunday mornings, if that's what he wanted to do. He was that good-looking. I planned to marry him as soon as I grew up, and spent part of each Sunday morning deciding which wasting-away disease would take his first wife out of the picture just in the nick of time. That week I favored leprosy, a fine biblical ailment.

"Turn to Luke 6:27," he continued. I saw Suzie fumbling with Mama's Bible, looking for the passage; my smile was smug. "Love your enemies; do good to them which hate you; bless them that curse you; pray for them which despitefully use you." I thought about that. *Whew.* I'll admit I hadn't spent any time praying for Kat Barrington. I mostly just stayed out of her way if I could.

She liked playing with me, for some unknown reason, but I think she liked despitefully using me even more.

Brother Dimmesdale went on to say that the college students protesting the war in Vietnam were fighting for peace, which confused me because Daddy always said the boys Walter Cronkite showed us on the six o'clock news were long-haired, dope-smoking draft-dodgers, and Mama said the girls were loose women who burned their bras and had no names for their babies, and I didn't know how they could all three be right.

"And unto him that smiteth thee on the one cheek, offer also the other," the preacher read on. Mama was a face-slapper when she was mad, and the last thing I wanted to do when she slapped me was tempt her to slap me again. Being a good Christian sure wasn't for sissies!

Six

At home, late that night, I lay in bed, awakened by angry voices coming through the thin wall that separated my room from my parents'. For people who seemed so perfect at church, taking in orphans and such, our family had its share of secrets during my childhood years, one of which was the amount of time my parents spent arguing. Suzie, evidently a deep sleeper, snored softly beside me and didn't budge. I guess she'd learned to sleep soundly surrounded by the noise made by all the other children at the Baptist Home.

"Now that we have another mouth to feed, why can't I get a part-time job, so we can paint the house and go on a nice vacation?" Mama asked.

"No wife of mine is getting a job, that's why," Daddy said, in his *and that's final* voice. "We painted the house two years ago, it still looks fine. And don't I always take y'all camping down at Strickland's Landing every summer?"

"That's my point. I'm tired of camping! I want the kids to see Washington, D.C. I want to stay in nice hotels."

My stomach hurt. I liked camping out. Why was Mama being so mean? This was clearly all Suzie's fault—I knew we couldn't afford another kid!

Daddy's voice went up a notch. "Well, let's just get a divorce, then you can get your precious job, or find a man who can afford fancy hotels. But get one thing straight, Rose Lee—you won't be taking *my* children with you."

Divorce! No, Daddy, no! They wouldn't really, would they?

"They're *my* kids, too! Who do you think's gonna watch the little house apes and clean up after them, besides me? Kids belong with their mother."

I shivered to think of living with Mama without Daddy, and then curled up in a ball on my side, pulling the covers up tighter, trying to get warm. It was late spring, warm in Florida, but their yelling made me cold all over.

Who would I live with if my parents got divorced? Mama could never get along without me, and I'd die if I couldn't see my Daddy every day.

"Then straighten up and fly right."

Yes, Mama, I thought. Straighten up and fly right. Our house looked fine. Camping out was fun.

"I don't know why I ever promised till death do us part!" Mama shouted.

"That's always an option," Daddy yelled back. "I've got a pistol. Don't tempt me."

Cold silence was Mama's reply.

Oh, Lord, now they were talking murder.

How in the world could I make this better? I decided I'd help Mama out more around the house, be less sassy. Maybe then she wouldn't be so hard on Daddy.

"I promise to do better, Jesus, if you won't let them get divorced," I prayed. This would be a great time to be able to work miracles, I thought.

I stared at the little stuffed bird, covered in real feathers, hanging from the light fixture over Suzie's head and mine, in a wispy cage Mama had made out of purple pipe cleaners and lavender tulle. "Don't be scared, don't be scared, don't be scared," I chanted to it in the dark.

This whispered litany reminded me that Kat Barrington, a Catholic, had shown me how to curtsy and make the sign of the cross one time when I visited with her family during mass. She called it genuflecting.

In contrast to the simple services at Beverly Hills Baptist Church, Kat's mass had been a lush affair at Our Lady by the Sea. The priest must have had a sense of humor, however. The cathedral was located in a neighborhood of streets named after various fish, in keeping with its seaside location. On the west side of A1A, the street sign read Mackerel Lane, but on the east side, the church side, the street sign bore the name Holy Mackerel.

While the Barringtons and other Catholic worshipers genuflected at the font of holy water, I'd busied myself taking in the crucifix, the rose window, the stained glass, the gleaming pipe organ, the incense, and the army of pulsating candles doing war with the shadows. The setting alone felt holy.

I lingered in the foyer by a rack of colorful cards with pictures of martyred saints on the front, their stories on the back. I took one of each and then, taking a seat in a pew beside Kat, carefully read through the entire stack, shuffling them like an Old Maid deck, while all around me people stood and sat, knelt and prayed, ate the bread and drank the wine. Music rose and fell; voices did the same. I was confused about what to do when, but tried to follow Kat's lead. I loved it when she showed me how to cross myself.

As we filed from the church, I left all the cards on the seat, except one. Saint Joan of Arc, wearing a white suit of armor, riding a black stallion, lifted her banner high. A quote beneath her picture read: "Doubt not. Work and God will work also." The biography on the back of the card said that when she was just a few years older than me, Saint Joan, dressed as a boy, led the French army against England and, despite being shot with an arrow to the throat, a cannonball to the head, and a bolt from a crossbow to the thigh, she saw village after village returned from British to French rule, and the French prince crowned king, just as her "heavenly voices" had predicted. This girl-soldier was nearly indestructible. Even when they eventually executed her, they'd had to burn her body three times. They were that afraid she'd come back to life.

What was the secret to her invincibility? Two words that I whispered three times as I emerged into the sunlit courtyard of the church. "Doubt not. Doubt not. Doubt not."

Three was the number of the Trinity. Three was a magic number. Three times that Easter Sunday night I lifted my prayers past the little stuffed bird, past my ceiling, past the stars.

No divorce. No divorce. No divorce. Three times I made the sign of the cross.

Father, Son, Holy Spirit. Father, Son, Holy Spirit. Father, Son, Holy Spirit.

Amen. Amen. Amen.

The next morning, Mama and Daddy didn't talk much at breakfast, but at least they weren't tossing around the D-word or the M-word. I figured my prayers and the magic number three had done the trick, but maybe making the sign of the cross when you were Southern Baptist was a bad idea. Mama wasn't the only gal in our neighborhood with a temper, and the auburn-haired Irish-Catholic one I mentioned came looking for me later, once school was out for the day. Had my cross-faith experiment conjured up more trouble?

I heard a friendly knock at our kitchen door and threw it open to find Kat staring at me with her usual devil-may-care grin. She was only nine, like Suzie, but stood a head taller than me and outweighed me by thirty pounds. She was solid, raw-boned and gangly, with a big, shaggy mane of hair. I was little, skinny, and bookish, with a quick wit and a smart mouth, intelligent enough in what was called "book learning," but I lacked the common sense to keep my big mouth shut. Kat whipped my tail on regular occasion.

There was a severe shortage of kids in our immediate neighborhood, so Kat had been my only choice of a playmate until Suzie moved in. Most days I just read a book after school, or watched Dark Shadows on TV, with the vampire, Barnabas Collins, the witch, Angelique, and the werewolf, Quentin. But there my real-life monster stood, and I had nowhere to hide.

"Wanna come see what I got in my playhouse, Bee?" she ventured. She called me Bee, short for Honey-bee, and I called her Kat-with-a-K because she made me.

I mumbled something about homework and my cousin being here for a visit, but Mama piped up from the sink, where she was getting an early start on cutting up a chicken for supper. "Suzie and I need some one-on-one time. If I let Honey come out and play, do you promise not to whip up on her this time?" Mama didn't believe in beating around the bush.

I turned ten shades of red and screeched, "Mama!" as if that was the farthest concern from *my* mind, but Kat nodded her head vigorously and said, "I'll be real nice," while she reached out and took my free hand, the one I'd opened the door with. Mama took *Black Beauty* out of my other hand—she thought I read too much and was always pestering me to *put that book down and go outside and play*—and gave me a little push. I never admitted to Mama that sometimes I read just to escape her wrath, to keep silent and stay out of harm's way. A reading child is a quiet child.

But that afternoon it was clear that I was outnumbered.

"Be home by dark, Honey," Mama ordered, as if I didn't know that rule by heart. I was grateful she'd made her expectations clear, because Kat and I always had a pretty good time playing until I had to come home. She'd start pounding me whenever I tried to leave. I never knew loneliness could make someone so mean.

My family lived in a little white frame house on the top of a hill that sloped down to the river. Bass River Road ran in front of our house, and made a cross with Ridge Road. We lived where Jesus' head would have been on that cross, and the Barringtons lived on the corner of Ridge Road, in Jesus' right armpit. It was saying such things aloud that got me all those lickings. In those days I still hadn't learned that not every thought that popped into my head had to come out of my mouth.

Still pulling me along by the hand, Kat did a left-right-left check for traffic, and then broke into a trot as we crossed our busy, winding street, notorious for speeders. I felt I was running toward my doom. We didn't slow down until we'd rounded the side of her house, where she dropped my hand and slung open the door to her playhouse. "Ta-DAH!" she trumpeted.

Kat's playhouse was a source of fame in our neighborhood. Her big sister Lucy had gotten a Volkswagen Beetle for her birthday the previous summer, and Kat got the wooden box the car was delivered in. The whole Barrington family had gone down to Mayport and picked up the new car straight from the ship. They used a great big crane to unload it onto a flatbed truck, then Kat and Lucy's daddy pried off one side of the box with a crowbar and the whole neighborhood stood around admiring the funny-looking little bug as Lucy proudly drove it down the ramp, tooting the horn all the way. She was supposed to watch her little sister while her parents worked, but she was never around much after that, always out joy-riding with friends her age, leaving Kat at home alone.

Once Kat's daddy added a red door, a window, and a peaked, shingled roof to the box the car came in, I speculated that Kat might have gotten the best end of the deal. Now that I saw what was waiting inside Kat's playhouse, I knew she had.

Santa Claus had brought Kat a waterbed last Christmas. That fact alone was enough to give her a certain notorious status in the neighborhood, since most of us Southern Baptists had never even seen, much less slept on, one of the things. Waterbeds were all tied up in our minds with hippies, drugs, and free love, which I was pretty sure meant having babies without benefit of a wedding. Now here the waterbed mattress lay, in all its sinful glory, on the floor of Kat's playhouse.

Kat let out a Tarzan yell and bounded into the middle of the waterbed. It sloshed delightfully, she staggered, and then lost her footing and fell with a plop, laughing.

"Won't it bust, Kat?" I asked.

"Naw, it's tough as alligator hide," she said.

So I did a belly-flop beside her, and we rolled around, making waves crest and fall below us.

"This is so cool!" I crowed, and she agreed. "How did you talk your folks into moving it out here?"

"It made me seasick to sleep on it," she said. "Every time I turned over at night, I nearly puked. But it sure is fun to jump on." So we did, again and again and again, taking turns stomping like elephants to send each other flying into fits of giggles. Then we'd lay where we fell, riding the waves and trying not to upchuck.

We barely noticed dusk falling, until I heard Mama's voice calling across the street, "HONEY! Supper!"

Mama was the only person I knew that I was more scared of than Kat, and she didn't like to have to call me twice, so I jumped up right away, trying to get my balance on the wiggling waterbed.

"I'd better get going," I began, but Kat cut me off. "You ain't going nowhere, Bee Lee. We ain't done playing." She stood, looming over me. She jumped and rammed her feet straight down, and I fell to my hands and knees on the waterbed.

I struggled to a jiggling stand once again. "But I have to be home by dark, Kat," I whined. "We've got company."

She stepped in between me and the playhouse door. "I'll tell you when you can go home," she said. Her frown was a cruel slash in the half-light from the street-lamp outside. Her hands balled into fists.

Desperate, I made a sudden lunge to the right, and slipped out the playhouse window, dropping a few feet to the ground below, which momentarily threw Kat for a loop. Small and wiry, I got a good head start, but Kat had much longer legs, plus she wore PF Flyers with the *run faster/jump higher* action wedge, like Johnny Quest. Once she'd thrown open the door and gotten moving, she was pretty fast. She caught up with me at the curb, where she grabbed one of her family's metal garbage can lids. She banged me on the head with it as I ran for home.

Run, *whack!* Run, *whack!*

Although it was just across the street, home had never looked farther away.

Mama stood on our kitchen steps, hollering, "Honey, are you fighting?"

"No, Ma'am," I yelled back. "I'm running!"

When Kat saw Mama, she put on the brakes.

I didn't have that choice. I tried to scoot around Mama on the carport steps, but she snatched my left arm with a hand like a claw, stopping me cold.

"Don't you lie to me! I saw y'all fighting. And didn't I tell you to be home by dark?" she hissed. She yanked my arm, and her talons sank deeper into my flesh.

"Oww!" I blurted, trying to wriggle away. Her grip tightened. It pinched.

"You think you can make up your own rules around here, do just what you wanna do?"

The words spilled out before I could stop them. "I didn't want to go over there! You made me!"

Mama's lips twisted into a sneer. I didn't see the slap coming till it landed across my mouth. "Don't you sass me!" My head jerked back; my eyes stung and watered.

"Stop that crying." she snarled.

I hung my head and blubbered. It wasn't fair! "Do you want me to give you something to cry about?"

I shook my head. *Why did she hate me so?*

"Do you?" Her nails felt like snake-bites. "No, Ma'am. I'm sorry, Mama."

Her grip loosened a little. She gave my arm a push. "Go wash your face, and get to the table. You're holding up supper."

I knew enough to eat Mama's delicious fried chicken and not talk, once we all sat down at the table. Daddy could see I was in trouble with Mama, and I guess he was still mad from their fight the night before, so he didn't say much. He looked as miserable as I felt. Suzie watched us all with her big black eyes, saying little beyond *please pass this* and *may I have more of that*. Jimmy did most of the talking, and most of the eating.

After supper, Suzie went to take a bath while Jimmy washed the dishes and I dried. I broached the subject of him beating up ol' Kat for me.

"Boys don't fight girls, Little Bit, even if they deserve it."

"I know, I know, 'Blessed are the peacemakers,' right?"

"Actually, unless you enjoy shame, you need to stand up to her, instead of running away," he explained, as if that strategy wasn't easier said than done. His eyes were Tootsie-Roll brown, like mine and Daddy's, and they crinkled as he smiled at me. "There's another Bible story you need to think about—David and Goliath."

I considered that while I dried the silverware and put it away in the drawer and he scrubbed the pots and pans. "It's just that, she's so big and mean, she scares me," I finally confessed.

"I know, Bit. But courage isn't about not being scared. It's about being scared, yet still doing what you know you have to do." He grinned, and did his judo bow, with his hands on his knees. "That's what my sensei says."

I did the judo bow right back, giggling, and thought about what he'd said as I swished the dish-towel around and inside Mama's dripping black cast-iron frying pan.

That night, I dreamed that a shepherd boy handed me his slingshot, and we both cheered when I aimed straight and true and a great monster thudded to the ground. But when we turned the giant over to make sure it was dead, I saw that it was Mama's creamy forehead, not Kat's, I had cracked open with the smooth, white stone.

Seven

From day one of Suzannah's years with us, Mama made me jealous, the way she fussed over her beauty.

"You're a ring-a-ding doozie and a black-eyed-Suzie," she'd say. This always made Suzie laugh. Black-eyed Susans, just a roadside weed, were suddenly my mother's favorite flowers, and Suzie made sure she picked enough of them so that Mama always had a fresh bouquet on the kitchen table.

She wasn't just pretty on the outside, either. That would have made her tolerable. If she'd been peevish or shallow, I'd have had an excuse to dislike her. But it seemed like the rougher this old world treated her, the kinder Suzannah felt about the world and the people in it. I didn't understand her attitude at all. Once in a while, I'd even find myself thinking she wasn't half bad, if I had to have a baby sister.

Every night she was with us, Suzannah talked about one thing, nonstop, when we turned out the lights and tried to fall asleep—how great it was going to be when, any minute now, her dad stopped drinking, her mom snapped out of whatever strange world she lived in (Suzie called it "getting better") and they all would be one big, happy family again. I might have been only ten when she came to live with us, but even I knew it was bull. Uncle Travis loved his beer more than his girls, and Aunt Rita Faye just wasn't able to care for her young'uns.

Uncle Travis and Aunt Rita Faye rarely called to check on their girls, even though the aunts tried hard to make sure the three sisters saw each other most weekends at one or the other of their houses, or at least said goodnight to each other on the party-line.

One night when I felt particularly cranky, I shared these thoughts with Suzannah. She stared at me with solemn eyes from the other side of our big double bed.

"My parents are my parents and I love them. I'll be ready to go home with them and my *real* sisters the minute they come for me." She looked fierce.

Her expression shut me up. She was usually so calm. I guess I was kidding myself that we were ever going to be sisters. I was good enough to share a bedroom, a bathroom, and a family with, but I'd never be more than a cousin in her mind.

After that, Suzie was quick to bristle if I mentioned her parents. Mama generally stuck up for her, too. Once, I got Suzie good, though. We were playing backyard touch football with some of Jimmy's friends at the neighbor's field, away from Mama's watchful eye. Suzie was on the other team and she had the ball.

Peacemaking was the last thing on my mind. I felt more like *Vengeance is mine, sayeth the Lord.*

Bigger and faster, I made a beeline for my unfortunate cousin and hit her hard. Take that, black-eyed Suzie!

There was a terrible "whooooof!" as the air rushed from her lungs. She fell flat on her back, the football went flying, and we all started to laugh.

My heart sang, *Oh, Suzannah, won't you cry for me?*

Suzie didn't get up. She wheezed and gasped for air.

Her big, chocolate eyes got bigger and blacker. Jimmy punched me hard on the shoulder.

"Lookit what you did, you idiot!" he said. "You've gone and killed her!"

I got terribly scared. Was she going to die? Had I killed my cousin because she was prettier and sweeter than me? Maybe I was a murderer, just like Paw Paw.

I screwed my eyes tight and prayed, harder than I'd ever prayed before.

Lord Jesus, please heal little Suzie. I'm sorry, Lord. I'll never be mean to her again. Just please, please, please, make her okay.

You only needed faith the size of a mustard seed, right? I crossed myself three times.

Father, Son, Holy Spirit. Father, Son, Holy Spirit. Father, Son, Holy Spirit.

I sat Suzie up and rubbed her back. "I'm sorry, Sooooze. I didn't mean to do it. I was just playing. Come on, you're all right."

Her breathing eased, and a little color returned to her gray face.

I brushed the leaves out of her hair, the dirt off her clothes. I helped her onto her bike. "C'mon, Suzie, I'll take you home."

She never told on me.

That's the thing that killed me about her. She'd been kicked around and had to know in some secret part of herself that she wasn't wanted by the two people she loved the most, but she just kept on loving—right through her anger. I didn't understand it. Her attitude toward her parents made me mad. But I sure did admire her. And I was grateful that her forgiving ways extended even to me. She was more like Corrie Ten Boom than I'd ever be.

When I got her home, I offered to make Suzie a fried egg sandwich, one of my favorites.

She said, "No, thanks," and shuddered. Seeing that I wanted to make amends, she confided, "When I was little, and Mama was in the hospital, we'd get a lot of nice food from the ladies at church or some of our neighbors, or your mama and the other aunts.

"But when Mama was home, taking care of us, all she knew how to cook was fried eggs."

"That doesn't sound too bad," I joked. "I love me some fried eggs."

Suzie didn't laugh. "Think about it. Three meals a day, seven days a week, of fried eggs. I'll eat anything you give me, gobble it down without complaint, and thank you kindly for it. But I can't abide the thought of fried eggs."

Still, Suzie was itching to go back, to that mother, to that kitchen. She was hungry and soul-deep starving to go back.

After that, I felt a lot better about sharing my own less-than-perfect mother.

A few days later, it was gentle Suzie who came up with a way for me to skin ol' Kat. Turns out my cousin had been a little confused about me being such a roughneck with her, but such a chicken where Kat was concerned. She'd been puzzling on it.

Suzie was helping me vacuum the mats at the Benny Davis Judo Club where Jimmy took lessons, a twice-weekly chore earning me the princely sum of two dollars. I'd promised her one of the dollars if she'd do half the work of dragging the wheezy old black canister vacuum around what felt like forty acres of sweaty gray gym mats. I was explaining the system of colored belts a judo student earns, from white all the way up to black, when she interrupted me.

"If Jimmy is a brown belt, why don't you ask him to teach you some judo, so you can defend yourself against Kat instead of running?"

Of course! Boys didn't beat up girls, that was true, but there was no law against a boy teaching his sister how to tackle a bully, was there?

Suzie looked awful proud of herself. Who would have thought she'd have it in her?

My whole family gathered in our living room after supper that night, while Jimmy gave me a judo lesson.

"Now, Bit," he said, "all you really need to know how to do are two things: you need to know a good throw, and you need to know how to pin your opponent."

Mama looked worried. "I don't think it's very Christian to teach your sister how to fight. The Bible says to turn the other cheek."

Daddy shushed her. "Rose, Honey's turned every cheek she's got, and that gal keeps kicking 'um." Everybody laughed except me.

"Honey's David, and Kat's Goliath," offered Suzie.

Mama smiled. If it was in the Bible, it must be okay.

"It's like in *Billy Jack*, Mama," Jimmy said. We girls looked at each other and grinned. We were too young to see the movie, but Jimmy had seen it seven times at the drive-in, and had told it to us so many times, we knew every scene by heart. "Lil' Bit has been a pacifist long enough. Now I'm gonna show her how to take her right foot and whomp Kat right upside the face with it."

"*And there's not gonna be a dang thing she can do about it!*" Suzie and I roared our cleaned-up version of the line from the movie.

Jimmy showed me how to use an attacker's forward momentum to pull her off balance, over my hip, and to the ground. He started by demonstrating on me, over and over, until I finally begged him to stop. Then he let me practice for a while. What a thrill it was, the first time it worked. He wasn't a very big guy, but he was six years older than me, and with this simple judo throw I was tossing him to the ground with very little effort. For once I felt more like Superman than Lois Lane.

"The most important thing you have to remember, once you've got your opponent down," he said, "is to fall on her and pin her before she can get up." I had no argument with that, and he spent the next half hour perfecting a choke hold on me. How excited I was, when I tried it on him. Although I was smaller and lighter, he couldn't get up.

For the next few days, I went around practicing on anyone who stood still for more than a few minutes. I threw and pinned my brother some more. I threw and pinned my daddy. I threw and pinned Mama (just once—she didn't like it much) and I threw and pinned poor Suzannah until I'm sure she regretted her bright idea.

Finally, we decided I was ready. Kat was sure surprised when I called her on the phone and sweetly asked if I could come over to jump with her on the waterbed mattress on her playhouse floor. She hadn't seen me since the garbage can-lid incident, and she probably thought she'd never see me again, now that I had my cousin available full-time to play with.

I asked if Suzie could come, too, so she could watch the fun, but Kat said no. She liked having me all to herself. And she didn't want any witnesses.

We jumped for half an hour, me in delicious anticipation, she in blissful ignorance.

"Well, Kat," I said, "I reckon I'd better get started home."

"Oh, you don't have to go yet," she said. "Your skinny old mama won't start hollerin' for ya for at least another half-hour."

"Don't call my mama names, Kat. Move out of my way, now. I'm going home."

Her look of surprise at my boldness was priceless. But it was nothing compared to her shock when she came barreling toward me and I grabbed the lapels of her button-up shirt, stuck my bony hip out, and threw her neatly, with a loud "SMACK!" onto the waterbed mattress.

Momentarily stunned that it had worked so perfectly, I almost forgot to pin her. Luckily, I remembered just in time.

I laid my scrawny body across her chest and pulled her shirt collar across her throat. Between the pressure of my weight on her chest and the collar gouging her windpipe, Kat was having a hard time breathing and found she didn't have much to say. Her blue eyes grew very broad. They were her most beautiful feature, and looking into them, filled with shock, gave me a delicious, terrible surge of joy.

I let her lay there and squirm for a bit. Then I offered to release her.

"I need to go home now. If I let you up, are you gonna give me any trouble?"

I loosened up on her collar just enough to let her talk.

Her face was crimson; she looked beyond furious. "Let me up so I can kick your butt."

I reapplied the pressure on her windpipe and lay there for a few beats more. She struggled heroically, but still couldn't move.

"Well, if you're gonna kick my butt, I guess I won't let you up."

I felt like Jacob wrestling with the angel, or the boy in that story who had a tiger by the tail. How to end this? I hadn't thought that part through. I began to worry that we'd both die there of old age, with Kat refusing to cry uncle, and me too scared to release her and make a run for it.

Finally, I asked again, in what I hoped was a reasonable voice, "I'm not having much fun here, and I know you ain't, either. I'd like to let you up now, and go home. Whaddya say?" I loosened the shirt across her neck. Her flesh had an ugly red mark on it that I guessed wouldn't go away for a day or two. Looking at it made me feel a little sick.

"Okay," said Kat. Her voice was quiet and meek.

Looking into her pretty blue eyes, I saw that she knew she was licked. There was something else in those eyes—a glimmer of respect. I pressed my advantage.

"Promise you won't call my mama names. And that next time we play, my cousin can play with us."

"Okay," she repeated.

I slowly untangled myself from Kat's body and stood.

Reaching out my hand, I helped her stand up. "Bye, Kat."

"Bye, Honey. See you tomorrow?"

A moment passed while I considered. "Okay," I said.

I wasn't sure we wouldn't have any more trouble, but I decided to hope for the best.

I walked home, feeling forty feet tall, humming *Joshua fi't the Battle of Jericho, and the walls came tumblin' down.*

Mama had the carport light shining for me.

Eight

Our house sat atop a hill so steep that we had three steps leading to our front door, six steps leading to the kitchen door on the side, and an even dozen steps leading from the den to our back yard. From the bottom of those steps, the slope gentled down to the banks of Bass River.

On those long, lazy Saturdays, as spring snuck up on my tenth summer, Kat, Suzie and I made a game of leaping from the back steps onto the grass below, sometimes landing on our feet, but most times breaking into a giggling roll down the hill. The one who could jump from the highest step was the winner. So far, Kat and I were tied on step ten. Her long legs couldn't make up for the fact that I was lighter, or that my victory in the playhouse had made me suddenly fearless. Suzie was afraid to go higher than step eight.

"I'm going inside now, to see what Aunt Rose is doing," she said.

"Call us when she gets lunch ready," I said. Mama had promised us grilled cheese sandwiches and Fritos corn chips.

After the door shut behind Suzie, Kat and I looked at each other and shook our heads.

"Chicken!" Kat said.

"Bless her heart," I responded.

The back of our house stood on cement block pillars stacked higher than our heads, and the builders had dug down into the side of the hill under the house to install a basement garage, with walls of cement block. The short, steep driveway made it hard to park a car in there, but the mossy slope was great fun to slide down in my white tennis shoes from K Mart. Kat tip-toed down, not wanting to get her fancy PF Flyers grubby.

Inside the garage was a dark, magical place for young girls to play. A single forty-watt bulb on a pull string hung from the middle of the room, which meant a spooky walk after we rattled the door up on its creaky rails. Sunshine didn't make it very far into the bowels of the cave, and we imagined all sorts of whispery, spidery, shivery things scuttling around.

The garage smelled of sawdust, paint, and mildew.

Mama called mildew, which grew in heat and moisture, the Florida state flower. It had gotten into the dusty stacks of old *National Geographic* magazines that lined one shelf, but a picture of bare-breasted African women with beaded rings around their long, slender necks and discs the size of bread plates in their ears and lips still fascinated us. We looked down our shirts at our own chests, flat as ironing boards, and turned to the next page. That one showed a photo of two men holding spears, wearing what looked like rolled-up diapers tucked into belts, which did nothing to hide their ebony butt cheeks. They shaded their eyes with their hands, watching the distant approach of an over-loaded, rickety bus kick up the sandy road into a red dust cloud.

"Well, you don't see that every day of the week," I said.

"Not at our bus stop," agreed Kat.

She'd grown a lot more agreeable in the weeks following judo night in the playhouse. I actually looked forward to her visits after that, and our family had taken her under our wing. According to Mama's philosophy, there was always room for one more at the Lee house. Kat turned bright red when she saw Jimmy, because he tugged her long hair whenever he walked past and said, "Meow, Kitty Kat." But I was used to all the girls, including our cousins, having crushes on my big brother, so it didn't bother me.

"What are those?" she asked, pointing to some canvases leaning against an easel in a dark corner. Tubes of oil paints, two messy palettes, and assorted brushes in mason jars littered the table beside the easel.

"Those are Daddy's paintings," I said. "Let's carry them under the light."

"I didn't know he was an artist!" she exclaimed. "I like to paint, too. But how does he do it down here in the dark?"

"He doesn't, silly. He takes his easel wherever he wants to paint. He just keeps it down here when he's not working on a picture. Mama doesn't like the mess, or the smell of paint in the house."

We thumbed through three or four florals and some paintings of birds. "These are good," Kat said.

"I know." I grinned. "You know the painting of the sailfish in our living room? Daddy painted that after reading *The Old Man and the Sea*. Didja ever read it? He thinks it's the best book ever, and I liked it, too."

"I don't like to read," she said, wrinkling her nose like she smelled something nasty.

Didn't like to read! I couldn't imagine such a thing. "Not even *Heidi*, or *Little Women*, or *Nancy Drew*?"

"I didn't like any of those," she said. "Hey, what's this?"

Kat walked back and reached under the cloth that draped the little table holding Daddy's paints. The corner of something jutted from its hiding place on the floor. She pulled it out and revealed a sketchbook, like one of many I'd seen Daddy carry over the years. *How did it get down there?* I decided he must have dropped it on the floor and then absent-mindedly kicked it under the table.

We sat on an old bench that had once matched our picnic table (the table itself was long gone) and thumbed through the sketchbook. Clipped at the top of each page with rusty paperclips were small water-color pictures of pin-up girls wearing swimsuits, high heels, and swept-up hair. It occurred to me why I'd never seen this particular sketch-book before, why it was tucked away, out of sight.

I remembered seeing that calendar hanging by the beer cooler in Paw Paw's store. Daddy had hardly ever been back there—he didn't drink beer.

Still, on each page of the sketchbook, in Daddy's unmistakable style, were pencil drawings of the pin-up girls from the little calendar. Some were faithful copies, some had the same lady in a different pose.

They were beautiful, half naked, and perfect, and Daddy had drawn them all. Kat looked at me and said what I was thinking. "Your mama's not going to like this one little bit."

I slammed the book shut and slid it back into its hiding place under the table. "That's why she can never find out. We can't never, ever tell, or they'll get a divorce." The one thing I wanted most in life was for our family to be together forever.

She took my hand and squeezed it. "I won't tell nobody, not a soul, *ever.*" She zipped her lip with her finger and thumb, turned the imaginary key, and poked at the pocket of her blue jeans. "Zip-it, lock-it, put it in my pocket," she intoned.

A sacred vow.

To distract us from the awful possibility of Mama ever finding that sketchbook, or Daddy knowing we'd peeked at it, I moved to the stack of *Florida Times-Unions* we were saving in a cardboard box for our school's newspaper drive. The one on top, dated May 5th, showed a photograph of a kneeling teen-aged girl with her arms spread out like Jesus on the cross. She was hollering over a boy who lay face down on the street as other kids walked past, watching.

"Massacre at Kent State," the headline screamed.

The photo was so dramatic, I knew Jimmy would want to see it. I'd take it upstairs and show it to him. He might even cut it out and hang it on his bedroom wall, next to *The Kiss of Life*.

"What happened?" asked Kat.

Feeling worried and cranky about the secret sketches, I shoved the paper at her. "Read it and we'll find out," I demanded.

She glanced at the page. "Mass ..." she began. "... ask her at Kate Street." She shoved the paper right back. "It doesn't make sense," she said.

"Massacre at Kent State," I corrected her. "Somebody killed that dead boy on the ground there." I read the first couple of paragraphs silently. The National Guard had shot some college students protesting President Nixon's invasion of Cambodia, a country near Vietnam, I explained. They were mad about being drafted to fight in the war, too. I looked up at Kat. Her face was bright red, and it suddenly hit me. She didn't *dislike* reading. She *couldn't* read. Nine years old and she couldn't read, something I'd been doing since Jimmy taught me when I was three.

Kat squinted at me as she realized I'd guessed her problem. I started mentally measuring the distance to the door, my only escape route, in case the old, killer-Kat showed her ugly face.

"Don't start acting like Lucy, always bossing me around and telling me I should read more," she growled.

No wonder she was mean to folks. What a secret to have to carry around!

It occurred to me that this was something I could help with, a project that could even be fun.

"Hey, Kat," I said. "School will be out for the summer soon, and we won't have much to do all day. What if we *played* school? I could start out being the teacher—ya know—help you with reading and stuff."

Her blue eyes blazed and her fingers curled into fists by her sides. I saw a flash of the old, defiant Kat. "I can read good. I just don't like to."

"I know," I said, feeling bad about embarrassing her. "It's okay. We don't have to play school if you don't want to."

She nodded and her hands relaxed. We heard the back door open and shut, then a thud as Suzie leapt down the steps. Kat pulled the string to turn out the garage light, and we walked up the slippery drive to find Suzie lying in the grass, laughing.

"Step Nine, you guys. Step Nine!

Kat gave her a hand up. "Way to go, Squirt," she said.

"Show us again," I said, skeptical.

So she did.

As we clapped and yelled "Hooray!" the back door opened. Mama's head popped out. "Done ate all the grilled cheese myself," she teased. "Reckon I should start on the Fritos?"

"No, ma'am!" we yelled, clambering up the stairs.

As we washed our lunch down with red Kool-Aid, Kat bragged to Mama and Jimmy about how Suzie had moved up another step on the stair-leap game.

Jimmy smiled at our cousin. "Sensei says that everyone has things they're good at, and things they're not good at. He says if you're not good at something, or if something scares you, you shouldn't let it conquer you. *Face your fear, and the death of fear will come.*"

I recalled that the last time he'd sounded like this was when he'd talked me into standing up to Kat. I didn't think I should bring that up with her sitting across the table.

"I'm going to go for step ten tomorrow," Suzie promised. She took a big bite of her sandwich.

Kat spoke up, eager to impress my big brother. "Honey's not all that good at art," she said. "I told her we could play school this summer, and I'd be her art teacher, show her how to draw and paint and stuff. I get all As in art at school."

My mouth fell open. Kat blushed and stammered, "And she's gonna pretend to teach me how to read all those hard books she likes."

Mama smiled. "What a great idea."

"And Suzie here is gonna teach us all to fly. I'll bet you gals will be jumping off Step Twelve in no time," Jimmy predicted. He grinned and swiped the last Frito from Kat's plate. She beamed like she'd just won the Best of Show blue ribbon at the art fair.

The next Saturday, when Daddy suggested that we visit the Cummer Museum of Art and Gardens, I remembered Kat liked art and suggested we take her along. Dressed in Sunday afternoon finery, a whole day early, we strolled through one of our family's favorite haunts. The museum was a special treat that could be enjoyed by all of us for a small donation.

My father, being an artist himself, had a special affinity for floral still lifes. I held his hand as we stopped in front of a stunning, ornate oil painting of a vase filled to overflowing with exotic and beautiful flowers. It was taller than Daddy.

"What do you see, Kat?" he asked my friend, who had confessed to him that she loved to paint, like he did.

"Flowers."

"What kinds of flowers?"

"Pretty flowers. Pink ones, white ones, peach and red ones."

"What are their names?" He waited.

I helped her out, conjuring names from my walks with Mama in her garden. "Roses, tiger-lilies, daisies, gardenias."

Daddy grinned, clearly pleased. "Look at that rose. Tell me about it." Kat and I leaned close to the canvas. It took us a while, and then we saw it. A tiny, perfect sphere of water, balanced at the arc of a blush-colored petal, eternally poised to slide down, down the dusky rose and plop onto the tablecloth below.

Kat squirmed, almost falling into the painting, pointing.

"Suzie, look. A dewdrop! Miz Rose, Jimmy, come see!"

Daddy smiled his satisfaction. Kat looked so excited I tried not to mind him paying so much attention to her.

The art museum boasted impressive English and Italian gardens sloping down to the St. Johns River. Because we were very, very good inside the galleries, Mama and Daddy treated us to a walk in the gardens. It was worth waiting for, especially the long, narrow terraced fountain that spanned the length of the grounds. After we ran around a bit, stretching our legs and filling our lungs, Mama called us over to where she and Daddy sat on a bench under a majestic live-oak tree.

"Ain't that pretty?" she pointed. On the base of the tree, at a perfect height for an inquisitive child to practice her reading skills, was a burnished bronze plaque. Written on the plaque were words I've never forgotten—my first ever grown-up poem:

TREES

I think that I shall never see
A poem as lovely as a tree....
Poems are made by fools like me
But only God can make a tree.

~ Joyce Kilmer

Suzie and I silently read the poem, but Kat barely glanced at the plaque before turning her attention to Jimmy, who balanced precariously on the wall that separated the gardens from the river. "Let's go wall-walking," she said, and Suzie scampered off with her.

"Get down, Son!" Daddy ordered. "You're setting a bad example for the girls. Now they want to try it. One of y'all is bound to fall in the river." Jimmy hopped down from the wall, but didn't look happy about it.

Poetry ran away with my heart that day. I memorized the poem where I stood and recited it again and again, to anyone who would listen. Even Doodle the Poodle. And when they didn't want to hear it anymore, I said it to myself.

That night, as I drifted off to sleep, the last thing I saw with my mind's eye was a tiny painted dewdrop on the petal of a rose.

Part Two

1972

Nine

It wasn't all poetry and roses for our family back then. By the time I turned twelve, Mama and Daddy's arguments had gotten so noisy and frequent that Jimmy, Suzie and I almost got used to them. A deficit of money and a surplus of jealousy were the two main catalysts, but almost anything, from clothes dropped on the floor to a toilet seat left up, would suffice to incite World War Lee. They usually got cranked up on Friday nights, and the dark joke between us kids, when we heard the first swell of angry voices from somewhere in the house, was, *Well, it's the weekend.*

Daddy bought a Honda 100 motorcycle and gave Mama, Kat, Suzie, and me rides on the back. Mama climbed off after her one and only ride, looking scared and queasy, but didn't make a fuss about him taking us for rides as long as we wore the spare helmet. "Be careful," she'd bark as we putted off down the road, waiting until we'd rounded the bend and she could no longer see us before picking up speed. She even let Daddy teach Jimmy to drive the bike, but put her foot down about Suzie or me learning. I wanted to drive that Honda by myself so bad I could taste it. "Nice girls don't drive motorcycles," Mama declared, and *that was that.*

Daddy was just as unreasonable about my other wish: to get my ears pierced. On a soft spring afternoon in April, Mama and I picked up the cutest little fourteen carat gold studs on sale at the Pic N' Save, and I wanted to go straight home, ice up my earlobes, and stick a needle through them, like all the girls at Highlands Junior High were doing. Even Suzie and her sisters had pierced ears. But Mama foolishly waited to ask Daddy's opinion, and he bristled right up. "No daughter of mine is going to have pierced ears," he intoned. All evidence that I was the only female in Jacksonville who still hadn't had her ears pierced by 1972 made no difference to him whatsoever. Evidently, pierced ears were the first step on a slippery slope that led straight down to the Pits of Despair, and Daddy was going to protect me from it at all cost. Mama dropped the subject and put the little brown bag with the earrings and receipt on the table in the kitchen, to be returned the next time we went to the Pic N'Save.

The next Saturday, Daddy woke me up early by slipping into my room and grabbing hold of my foot, which always seemed to escape from the covers during the night to dangle over the side of the bed, until I opened one eye, yawned, and stretched. Suzie rolled over, stealing all the covers as she burrowed more deeply into her dreams.

"Let's go, Easy Rider," he snarled, trying to make his voice sound like Jack Nicholson's, and failing entirely.

He waited on the carport while I changed from pajamas to shorts and a tee-shirt, used the bathroom, and brushed my teeth, and then together we pushed the Honda up the driveway to the road, where he finally cranked it up, so as not to wake Mama and the rest of the household.

I stood on a foot peg and slung one leg over the back of the seat, settling in behind Daddy. We strapped our matching plain white helmets on our heads, and I grabbed his shoulders as we took off down Bass River Road.

Generally we stuck to the back roads and made a big, sloppy loop along the river and through the dairy farms, but today Daddy went left instead of right, and drove only a few miles before we passed Paw Paw's store and crossed a small bridge over Bass River. He turned into the entrance of the Junior College and pulled around to the most remote section of the parking lot in back before stopping the bike and taking off his helmet. There were no classes this early on a Saturday morning, and we had the place to ourselves.

"Climb down, Honey," he said, so I did.

He dismounted as well, and stood the motorcycle on its kickstands.

"Now, if you're going to learn to drive this thing, the first thing you need to understand is how big and powerful it is," he said.

"REALLY, Daddy?" I squealed. I hopped up and down and clapped my hands like a little kid. I was so excited, I couldn't help it.. Then my shoulders slumped. "I can't. Mama'll kill us both."

Daddy looked around the deserted parking lot. "Is your mama here?" he asked. I shook my head and grinned. "I won't tell if you won't," he said, and winked.

First, Daddy explained all the parts of the bike to me with the motor off. When I was able to repeat back to him where everything was, and its function, he had me lift the kickstands and roll the bike across the parking lot while walking beside it. He was right; the motorcycle weighed a lot more than I did, and I had to use all my strength to keep it upright. Daddy walked on the other side of the bike, just in case I couldn't hold it up, so I was proud that he didn't have to catch it.

Finally, he had me climb onto the bike and start it up. I felt exhilarated and terrified at the same time. Exhilaration won. I eased out the clutch like he'd shown me, gave it a little gas, and away I rolled. Almost at once, I squeezed the brake, and felt the bike respond by slowing down. It stalled out. I put my feet down on the ground, and Daddy ran up beside me.

"That's okay. Start'er up again," he said. He was smiling, proud. I wasn't as scared the second time, and when I drove away, Daddy couldn't keep up, even though he went from walking to jogging to running beside me.

The white lines that marked the parking spaces clip, clip, clipped by, and the pine trees lining the parking lot began to blur. The wind felt sweet against my cheeks. Thrumming beneath me was more power than I'd ever felt, and it was completely within my control. I laughed, and the roar of the engine swallowed the sound.

I didn't see the sand until afterward. All I knew was that the pine trees turned sideways—*wasn't that odd?*—and then the bike's wheels weren't under me anymore, but the asphalt was, and the weight of the bike crushed me and then *hot, oh Jesus, HOT* on my bare leg, and Daddy screamed *Honey* from a long way away, and I wanted him to come help, but though I heard the pounding of his shoes, it took forever and a day, and then he lifted the hot and the heavy off me and I thought *Thank God* just before the dark came down and I heard a howling noise that I thought came from him but it turned out to be me.

We putt-putted up our driveway, half-hoping Mama was still asleep and that we could somehow keep my burned shin hidden until it healed, but knowing better.

Daddy half-carried me up the steps and then I hopped on my good leg across the kitchen. Mama jerked out a chair from the table, and I plopped into it. Might as well face the music while Daddy was there to sing backup.

"What in the world —" Mama started, but Daddy interrupted.

"I was teaching her to ride. She hit some sand, and the muffler stung her."

Mama crouched beside me and took a long, close look at the wound. "That'll leave a pretty scar," she said.

And that was it. Not another word.

She bustled around the house, fetching goopy medicine and a clean, soft bandage roll that she loosely wrapped around my leg and fastened with white tape. It hurt a lot when she touched my shin, but I felt too guilty about my disobedience to complain more than a whimper.

Daddy stood behind my chair, chastened, waiting, like me, for the other shoe to drop, for the tirade to begin.

Mama busied herself making toast and putting a pot of water on the stove to boil. I assumed she was going to cook eggs. Daddy gave me a nervous smile before patting my shoulder and making his escape back outside to put the bike and helmets away. I hoped he'd come back right away, but he dawdled. I didn't blame him.

Now I'll catch it, I thought, but Mama just moved to the refrigerator for Daddy's medical equipment, like she did every morning after he ate his breakfast, using a set of tongs to lower the metal "gun" and glass syringe into the pot of boiling water on the stove. It's how she sterilized them back then, so Daddy could take his shot for diabetes. She'd boil the implements for a few minutes, then scoop them up with the tongs and lay them on a clean dish towel on the counter. After they cooled, Daddy would come in and draw insulin from a tiny glass vial with the plunger, then place the syringe into the gun. With the needle touching the skin of his upper arm, thigh, hip, or stomach, he'd trip the gun's switch, and it would poke the needle under the surface of his skin so the insulin could be pushed through the needle with the plunger. The muted thump always made me jump as if I was the one getting stuck.

Mama buttered her toast and slathered on apple jelly.

She put one slice on a small plate for me, poured me a glass of orange juice, and then ate her other slice of toast while leaning against the counter.

"Mama," I ventured. "I'm sorry I drove the motorcycle."

"What's done is done."

I almost fell off the chair. Could Daddy and I really be getting off so lightly?

Mama fished the gun and syringe out with the tongs and laid them out on the dish towel. Steam rose from them. "Your daddy and I agreed you couldn't drive the Honda, and he went against his word."

It sounded like Daddy was in plenty of hot water. My hurt leg throbbed under the bandage. Doodle wandered up and licked my ankle while I finished my juice. I thought about what I could say to cause her to make peace with Daddy while I watched Mama put the syringe into the gun.

Wait. Something wasn't right.

"You forgot the insulin, Mama," I said.

She moved toward me, needle held high in her right hand. "No, I didn't."

With her left hand, she grabbed my earlobe, tugging, and even as I flinched and tried to pull away, she poked the needle in and pressed the switch. *WHUMP.*

Pain coursed through my head. Hot tears blinded me. I shrieked.

"Oh, HUSH," she said. "If you're big enough to drive a motorcycle, you're big enough to stand a little poke."

She tore open the little brown bag on the table and retrieved one of the tiny gold stud earrings. Tilting my head to the side, she stuck the post through the hole she'd just made. I winced, but bit my bottom lip to keep from yelping.

"Can I put some ice on it before we do the other one?" I begged. I was almost a teenager, and I understood the strange politics of my parents' marriage enough to know that Mama had the upper hand, based on Daddy's earlier mistake. She was furious, but for once I was going to benefit.

I squeezed the lobe of my other ear between two cubes of ice, my hand still shaking from the shock of her sudden inspiration on how to get even with Daddy. I felt a little guilty, as if I were betraying him, but hey, he could have stayed inside if he'd wanted to stop us, and he was the one who'd started this tit for tat little game they were playing.

At least that's what I told myself.

Before my ear was good and numb, Mama shot a hole in that one, too. It didn't hurt nearly as much as her earlier sneak attack. But her squinted eyes and pursed lips still looked creepy. I suddenly understood the phrase: *Hell hath no fury like a woman scorned.*

Once both gold studs were in my ears, Mama reminded me I'd have to turn them several times a day to keep the holes from closing up. "And bathe them in alcohol," she instructed. "That leg's likely to get infected and fall off; you don't want your ears to fall off, too." She grinned, as if relishing the prospect.

Then she opened the kitchen door and leaned out. "James," she sang, her voice all sugar and light. "Come take your shot!"

For the thousandth time, I wished for long, straight Cher-hair, anything but my childish pixie cut, something to hide my shiny gold earrings.

Ten

The burn on my leg from the hot muffler wasn't serious, but after it healed, it left a bright pink scar to remind me what happens to girls who disobey their mothers. It stood out like a neon sign when I wore shorts to go jogging with Daddy.

Diabetes meant he had to watch what he ate and get plenty of exercise. Daddy taught himself karate from books he checked out at the library, and after we watched Frank Shorter win the marathon on television at the Summer Olympics in Munich, he got interested in jogging. I liked to tag along, because it gave us a chance to talk one on one.

Some of the things we talked about were pretty grown-up, like the killing of eleven Israelis by Palestinian terrorists at those same Olympics. We had a hard time making sense out of that.

One evening Daddy bent over to lace up his tennis shoes so we could head out up Ridge Road past the church. Our jogging route formed a big rectangle that took us two and a half miles. Sometimes after he dropped me off back at the house, Daddy would run it again the opposite way, for a total of five miles.

I already had my shoes on, and was doing some exercises in the den from my *President's Council on Physical Fitness* book while I waited for Daddy. I'd gotten it way back in elementary school, but the basic exercises were easy and fun, and they got my blood pumping for our run. Suzie was in our bedroom, doing homework. Mama said she'd have supper ready by the time we got back. Through the doorway, I could see that Jimmy kept picking sliced carrots and cucumbers out of the bowl of salad Mama'd tossed, earning a look, then a slap on the back of his hand. He laughed, swiped one last carrot slice, and moseyed into the den.

On the television, Walter Cronkite announced that President Nixon had ordered B-52s to bomb supply dumps and petroleum storage sites at Hanoi and Haiphong.

"I hate this stupid war! Do you think it'll ever end?" I asked my family.

"Not while Tricky Dick is in office," said Jimmy. He had pieces of carrot stuck between his teeth.

"Jimmy!" Mama scolded from the kitchen. "That's not respectful."

"I didn't vote for the man, but President Nixon *has* cut troop levels by seventy thousand men," countered Daddy.

He tugged on each of his knee-high sports socks. I saw that they didn't match his shorts, which didn't match his tee shirt. Men were so sloppy.

"You're right, Mama, I don't respect him," said Jimmy. He turned to look at Daddy. "And he might be reducing troop levels, but those draft notices still keep going out."

"Respect the office of the President, even if you don't respect the man," said Mama.

Jimmy put his hands on his hips. "We turn eighteen, and we're old enough to kill people with guns, just not old enough to drink or vote." He shook his head in disgust.

"Won't be any drinking in this house, no matter how old you get," Mama countered. She waved the knife in the air.

"Henry Kissinger says 'Peace is at hand,'" Daddy continued. "He's got North and South Vietnam discussing a cease-fire."

"From his mouth to God's ear," said Mama.

"Don't hold your breath," muttered Jimmy.

Daddy gave me a hand up from the floor, where I'd finished doing sit-ups, and we went outside to start our run. The sun was setting, round and red. The evening air felt cool and clean. The scent of a barbecue grill firing up behind some neighbor's house wafted our way.

"Why is Jimmy so mad at President Nixon?" I asked.

We waited for some cars to race pass, then crossed Bass River Road and began a slow jog up Ridge Road.

"He listens to that Bob Dylan and those other hippy freaks," Daddy said. "Your Mama and I are worried about him joining one of those gangs protesting the war, instead of buckling down and going to college."

"He told me he wanted to jump right in taking great news photos rather than wasting time going to college," I said.

Daddy harrumphed. "If he went to college, he'd get a good job and a draft deferment."

We ran past the Barrington house and waved at Kat's daddy, who always insisted I call him Uncle Billy, even though we weren't related. He stopped sweeping their sidewalk for a minute to wave back.

I called Kat's mama Aunt Pat, though she pronounced it "Ain't" Pat, with an Alabama twang. I always wanted to ask, "If you ain't Pat, who are ya?" but thought better of it, knowing she'd tell my Mama if I sassed her.

"Do you think Jimmy's scared of getting drafted?" I asked Daddy as we reached the judo club.

"All eighteen year-old boys are up for the draft," he said. "He's got no more to be scared of than anybody else."

We ran past the church. A riot of pink and white azaleas on each side gave it a festive air.

"Did you ever serve in the military?" I asked.

"I wanted to, but they don't take diabetics."

"Jimmy would say you were lucky, then."

"Well, let's hope his luck holds out," Daddy said.

"Maw Maw says we make our own luck."

"Your Mama would be happy if he'd make his own bed."

We ran faster. Nobody could make me laugh like Daddy could.

The knock came on a Tuesday afternoon. Jimmy was cutting the grass in the back yard while Mama trimmed her rose bushes. I tossed my pencil down on the kitchen table where Suzie and I were doing homework, glad to take a short break from math to answer the door.

The mailman stood on the other side of the screen. "I've got a letter for James Lee, Jr. He lives here, right?" I nodded. "Can you sign for it?" he asked.

"Sure," I said. Odd. Why didn't he just leave it in the mailbox, like always? Must be important.

The mailman gave me a clipboard. I signed on the line and wrote in the date. He took back the clipboard and handed me a stack of letters. I glanced at the return addresses. A bill from the Jacksonville Electric Authority. A bill from Southern Bell Telephone. An ad for car insurance. A letter for James A. Lee, Jr. from the United States Selective Service System.

I took Jimmy a glass of iced tea and the letter. The scent of fresh-mown grass and Mama's roses mingled; it smelled like the back door to Heaven. He wiped his forehead with his sleeve and drank the tea in four long gulps before he took the letter from my outstretched hand. "What's this?" he asked, but his face drained of all color when he saw who the letter was from. He grew still, but his hands shook as he ripped the envelope open.

He read the single page and shoved it back at me. "You didn't sign for this, did you?" he barked.

"Yes," I said, my voice small. "Was that wrong?"

He grimaced and said nothing, but jerked back to the idling mower and revved the engine to full throttle. He marched in straight lines, mowing neat rows in the sloping yard. I read the letter in my hand.

You are hereby directed to present yourself for Armed Forces Examination to the Military Entrance Processing Station named above to undergo a physical, mental, and moral evaluation. Registrants found to be healthy and fit will report for active military duty in June, 1973. Once notified of the results of the evaluation, a registrant will be given 10 days to file a claim for exemption, postponement, or deferment.

"Mama!" I yelled, and she dropped her pruning shears.

Jimmy had never flunked a test in his life. His armed forces examination was no exception. He was classified I-A—*Registrant available for military service.*

With the end of active U.S. ground participation in Vietnam, he was in the last wave of men conscripted. His luck had held out, all right. But it was the worst kind.

Eleven

In the weeks after Jimmy got drafted, when Suzie and I lay in bed at night, trying to fall asleep, there were three voices raised in anger down the hall. They went round and round the same tired arguments every night, without waiting for the weekend.

"This war is supposed to be winding down. Why should I go halfway around the world to kill people I have nothing against, in a war I don't believe in?" Jimmy asked.

"Because it's your duty as an American citizen!" Daddy yelled. Their voices sent chills through me, and I sat up, pulling on my bathrobe and sliding my feet into slippers.

"Because you'll go to jail for being a draft dodger, Son," Mama said.

"I'm a war resister."

"You're resistant to getting your hair cut short and saying 'Yes, sir,' is what you are," said Daddy.

"I'm resistant to getting shot or shooting anything other than a picture. I don't want to kill a man just because he's a Communist."

I slipped out of my bedroom, ignoring Suzie's scared expression, and crept down the hall toward the living room, where Mama, Daddy, and Jimmy argued.

"God will take care of you, Son. We can't lie down and let the Communists take over the world," said Daddy.

"Then you go kill them, Dad," said Jimmy, sounding weary.

"I would, if they'd let me."

I stood at the doorway. They noticed my presence, but it changed nothing. The fight raged on.

Mama chimed in. "If you don't report for duty, where will you go, Son? What will you do?"

"I can't tell you that, Mama."

"I'm your mother. You don't keep secrets from me." She was clinging to his arm with the eagle's talon grip I knew so well.

"What you don't know, you can't tell the F.B.I."

"So now you're Abbie Hoffman," Daddy sneered. I moved closer, put my hand on his shoulder. If Daddy noticed, he didn't show it.

"You'll be a fugitive." Mama chewed on her thumbnail. "How will you live? How will you eat?" She shook Jimmy's arm. "Answer me."

"There are people who will help me, Mama."

"Over my dead body!" shouted Daddy.

Jimmy turned and stared at him. "Better yours than mine, sir."

Daddy balled his fists. I jumped between the two of them and cried, "He didn't mean it, Daddy."

Daddy sagged; his hands relaxed. "Yes, he did."

Jimmy jerked his arm out of Mama's grasp and slipped out the door, into the night. My parents let him go.

"He'll be back," Daddy said. "He needs to cool off. Then he'll do the right thing."

"I just wish we knew what that was." Mama peered into the darkness, her face pinched.

Shortly before morning, a tap on my window awoke me. I tiptoed over, not wanting to awaken Suzie by turning on the light, knowing it had to be Jimmy outside. I pushed aside the curtain, and a glance out the window confirmed my suspicion. He motioned toward the back of our house, and I understood; he wanted me to open the back door. The air was wet; there was a slight drizzle. He slipped once, climbing the stairs.

I let him in, and we crept together to his room, where he threw a few things into his judo duffel. Doodle joined us, sniffing the bag, and I picked up the little dog and petted him to keep him quiet.

"Where are you going?" I whispered.

My brother closed his bedroom door and switched on his reading lamp. "North," he said, "or west. Not sure yet."

"How will you get there?"

He made a hitchhiking gesture. "With my thumb."

"How will you live?" I asked, echoing Mama.

"Maw Maw gave me some money. She doesn't believe in this dirty war, either." He showed me a fat wad of cash, circled by a thick green rubber band. I whistled softly.

"Don't tell," he said.

I shook my head. Of course not.

Jimmy looked around his small bedroom as if memorizing it. He moved to his turntable and lifted the last forty-five rpm record he'd listened to. He squinted at the label, and then thrust the disc into my hand. I looked down at Barry McGuire's "Eve of Destruction."

He wrapped me in a bear hug, tugged his Florida Gators baseball cap onto his head, patted Doodle the Poodle, and then slipped out the way he came.

I played the record Jimmy gave me so many times that day I lost count, even after Suzie begged me to stop, because it made her feel sad. I just stared at her for a second before turning the volume up louder. *There'll be no one to save / with the world in a grave ....*

Late that afternoon, I walked all the way to the bait and tackle store and cornered Maw Maw.

"Was Jimmy scared?" I asked. "Is that why he ran away?"

Maw Maw shook her head. "Someday you'll understand why it took more courage to leave than to stay and do what everyone expected of him when he thought what they expected was wrong."

She gazed out the store window at Bass River Road, as if she could see Jimmy out there, walking.

When Daddy got home from work that night, Mama grabbed his arm as soon as he walked in the door.

"Look here," she said, tugging him to see the muddy footprints and tracked-in leaves on Jimmy's bedroom floor. "His duffel is missing. I'm scared to death he's run off to Canada."

Daddy turned pale, but didn't say anything, just changed his clothes and then left the house to go for a run.

"Wait and I'll go with you, Daddy," I offered.

"Let your Daddy have some time alone to think," Mama ordered. "I need your help with supper."

We finished cooking, the table was set, and still Daddy hadn't returned. Mama watched the clock, her lips tight, saying nothing. As much as it scared me sometimes when Mama yelled, her tense silence was worse.

I couldn't stand it. I moved to the window and parted the sheer curtains. Daddy stood motionless at the edge of our driveway, near the street, staring at the house. "There he is!" I called.

"Go tell him supper's ready, girls," Mama said. Suzie and I raced out the door, both clamoring for his attention. Daddy didn't answer. He lurched toward us, making a low keening sound, and when he lifted his head, a string of drool reached from his chin to his chest. I grabbed his arm to keep him from falling while Suzie raced back to the house, screeching for Mama.

"Gah," Daddy said.

"Aunt Rose! Uncle James is *bad* sick! He's trying to say something, but he's not making any sense."

As Mama flew out the door, she called to me. "Honey! Call the emergency number. It's on a sticker on the phone, under the handset." While she eased Daddy to the grass, I did as I was told.

Stroke. That was the name for what had stolen my daddy's words.

The hospital chapel was quiet and cool, dimly lit along the walls, near the ceiling. My perch was a wooden pew halfway down the row, which stood before a wall of lovely stained glass lilies. In the left front corner there was a pulpit with a Bible lying open on it. In the right rear corner, by the door, was a kneeling bench. The air conditioner hummed.

I didn't read from the pulpit Bible. I'd brought my own, a small, well-thumbed King James version, yellow with gold filigree, which I'd grabbed at home before I rode with Mama to the hospital. It helped to have it with me. When I turned to it for comfort, it opened to Matthew 17:20, the spot I'd marked with the Joan of Arc saint's card from my visit to mass at Kat's church. "… for verily I say unto you, If ye have faith as a grain of mustard seed, ye shall say unto this mountain, Remove hence to yonder place; and it shall remove; and nothing shall be impossible unto you." That was Jesus talking. I knew this because the words were written in red ink. All the other words in the Bible were in black ink, even God's, starting with the very first thing He'd ever said out loud, "Let there be light," in Genesis 1:3. But the first four chapters of the New Testament, the gospels according to Saints Matthew, Mark, Luke, and John, were filled with wonderful red print. I liked to read those words and think that Jesus was talking straight to me.

Like an editor at a newspaper, I trimmed the verse to fit my needs. That day, as my father lay in a room just down the hall and around a corner from the hospital chapel, Jesus issued to me from the tissue-thin pages of my Bible both a promise and a challenge: "If ye have faith as a grain of mustard seed … nothing shall be impossible unto you."

I remembered the jar of mustard seeds our Sunday school teacher had in her purse. She'd shown them to us so we'd know just how little faith it took for God to work a miracle. I picked up the Joan of Arc card and read the magic words printed on the front: "Doubt not."

Jesus, please don't take my Daddy. I need him here with me.

Like Saint Joan, I had faith, and I trusted Jesus to deliver his part of the bargain.

Daddy did get better, and it was great to have him home. But Winn-Dixie wouldn't let him go back to work at the print shop until the doctor said he was completely healthy again, and Mama struggled to pay the bills with only his disability insurance check.

This time when Mama's Sunday school teacher mentioned that her brother-in-law was hiring at the JC Penney jewelry counter, Daddy didn't argue. He had no choice; we needed the money. Mama, to her credit, tried not to look too happy when she drove the Green Hornet off to work each morning. She promised her new job was only temporary.

On the other hand, the Vietnam War seemed like it might drag on forever.

We each missed Jimmy's presence in our own way, and found it painful to hear others speak about him. Soon they learned not to mention his name, and we spoke it among ourselves only in whispers. My brother was gone, like smoke, from our lives.

Part Three

1974

Twelve

During my childhood, Mama always worried that cigarettes and beer would kill her father. In May of my ninth-grade year, Paw Paw had surgery for lung cancer. They cut one whole lung and half of the other one out of him. Mama, Suzie, and I went to visit him in the hospital after school on Mama's day off, a week after the operation. Daddy was back to work at the Winn-Dixie print shop, but only part-time, so despite describing it as temporary, Mama had kept her job selling jewelry at Penney's.

It was a hot day, so Mama and Suzie slipped out of the room with Maw Maw to get us all some iced tea from the coffee shop downstairs.

I was wondering what to say to Paw Paw now that we were alone, when the odor of a fresh-lit cigarette wafted over the curtain separating his bed from his roommate's.

Paw Paw crooked his finger at me in a "come here" motion. I stepped closer to the bed.

"Look in that drawer." Paw Paw pointed at the nightstand. I opened the drawer to see his car keys and wallet. "Get a five-dollar bill out," he wheezed. I did as I was told.

"Take that downstairs to the gift shop, and tell the lady you want a pack of Marlboros," he whispered, giving me a wink. "Buy yourself a candy bar with the change."

I couldn't believe a man in his condition, with only half a lung left, wanted to smoke.

I shook my head. "They won't let me buy you cigarettes, Paw Paw. And Mama would kill me."

"She won't know if you hurry," he scowled.

"I'm only fourteen. They'll want to see identification, and I don't have my driver's license yet," I countered, sliding the money back into the drawer. I was pretty spooked, talking back to Paw Paw, but saw he was in no shape to do anything about it. I felt a surge of pride at my rational excuse. Mama would be proud.

Paw Paw didn't look proud at all.

A nurse's aide came in and swept aside the curtain that obscured the bed next to Paw Paw's. She fiddled around the patient's bed, plumping pillows, smoothing sheets, taking his temperature and blood pressure to record on a clipboard. The lower part of his face was half gone. I felt my own jaw drop.

Mama, Suzie, and Maw Maw sailed into the room with my iced tea. Maw Maw waved gaily at Paw Paw's roommate and said to me and Mama, "Earl here has had his larynx removed." She lowered her voice to a whisper. "Mouth and throat cancer."

The middle-aged man spoke by holding what looked like a little transistor radio over a tiny hole in his throat. "Hello, Ladies. Where's my tea?" His eyes were kind, as if he knew his lower face looked like a monster's, and he wanted to make up for it.

When he exhaled into that little mechanical box, he sounded like a robot. I thought that was kind of cool. But what he did next drove the cool factor right out the window. He could no longer manage it with his butchered-up mouth, so he stuck the unlit end of a cigarette into the tiny hole in his throat and inhaled mightily.

Even that wasn't the worst of it—when he exhaled, the smoke came out of that little opening where his voice box used to be.

Suzie and I exchanged horrified glances.

"Earl, it drives me crazy to smell that smoke. These witches won't let me take a single puff," Paw Paw grumbled. He gasped for breath between words.

The robot voice intoned, "Don't worry. Once they give up on you, they let you smoke all you want."

Up to that point, smoking had seemed silly and stinky to me, but I didn't have strong feelings about it one way or another, unlike Mama, who had added it to her long list of things-that-were-sinful.

Paw Paw had his own special ashtray to use at our house, and it was one of the great joys of my childhood to watch Paw Paw light up. The ashtray was run-of-the-mill cut glass, but Maw Maw had bought it at a garage sale and thought it was wonderful. The cool part was the molded plastic donkey that perched on one edge. When you lifted his tail, the donkey made a braying sound and pooped out a cigarette. If you pulled back his ears, he spit out a match.

You lit the match by striking it on the tiny saddle that sat on top of a striped Mexican blanket draped across the donkey's back.

But I vowed right then to never take the first puff.

Death would have to find another way to get me.

I guess Paw Paw didn't care too much for a life without cigarettes. He took a turn for the worse and died the same week, without ever leaving the hospital or taking another drag.

We kids had a hard time knowing how to feel about Paw Paw's death. He wasn't the kind of man you naturally felt close to, and the whispers we'd heard about women, booze, and possible early ties to the Ku Klux Klan were downright scary. Still, he was quick with a joke and generous with small gifts off the shelves of his store, and the contrast was hard to reconcile. Daddy said it was okay to love somebody even if you didn't like them all that much sometimes, and Mama just acted like somebody dying made up for anything they'd ever done wrong in their whole lives. Instant sainthood, courtesy of the grave.

Kat, Suzie and I talked about little other than the funeral for a while after it happened. It was our first death, and like most firsts, that made it memorable.

One afternoon a few weeks after Paw Paw's funeral, we three girls watched *Dark Shadows*, which played every weekday after school at three o'clock, and then decided to tape-record a spooky show of our own. We made it up as we went, frequently pressing the STOP button to deal with fits of giggles.

Kat had a sudden inspiration. "Honey, you lie down on the couch and play like you're dead. Suzie, run get the record player and that forty-five by Bobby Goldsboro."

Suzie balked. "If you're thinking of playing that 'Honey' song, think again. It makes me cry."

Kat gritted her teeth, a sure sign of trouble. "It's a funeral, dummy. You're supposed to cry."

No arguing with that logic. I took my place on the couch, grabbed a fistful of black-eyed Susans from the jug on Mama's coffee table, and held them, with folded hands, on my chest. I closed my eyes and practiced being dead while Kat and Suzie got the music ready.

Kat pressed RECORD. "Dearly beloved, we are gathered here to bury my dear wife, Honey."

I cracked open one eye. "Your *wife?*" Kat stomped her foot and pressed STOP on the tape recorder.

"That's what it says in the song."

"Sounds like I'm married to a sissy."

"Try making your voice sound deeper," Suzie suggested.

Kat pressed REWIND, then STOP, then RECORD. "Today, we send my beloved wife, Honey, to her eternal reward. Mr. Bobby Goldsboro is here to sing a song I wrote in honor of the occasion."

Suzie placed the needle on the record, and Kat sang along in her best fake baritone. "And Honey, I miss you …."

Suzie chimed in with the angelic-sounding background singers, getting so carried away with her oooOOO crescendo that I sat up as the song ended and said, "Guess what, Darling—I'm not dead."

Kat pushed me back down on the couch and said, "Yes, you are."

I sprang back up to a seated position. "No, really, I'm not."

She pushed me back down, grabbed a throw pillow, and held it over my face, laughing. "Yes, you really, really are!"

Suzie took the needle off the record and intoned solemnly into the tape recorder, "The deceased is looking a little restless. Undertaker, take'er under."

Kat and I both pelted Suzie with throw pillows from the couch.

"I'm gonna say that out loud at your funeral," I promised my cousin.

"Won't work," she said. "I plan to live forever."

"Good plan," Kat said. "Me, too."

I grew quiet, thinking of Daddy and his stroke. Paw Paw had probably thought he was immortal, too.

That night, Kat, Suzie, and I stood before the huge double doors of the Collinswood mansion, as fog rolled in from the shores of Collinsport. I realized I was dreaming about *Dark Shadows*, but still felt a chill as Kat's bone-white hand reached for the big brass knocker that we knew would summon Barnabas Collins.

"Kat, wait!" I shouted.

She ignored me, instead giving three loud raps, but Suzie turned to me with a sad smile. "We want to live forever, Honey. This is the only way."

The door creaked slowly open, and I saw the familiar sweeping black cape and wolf's head cane. But before he sank his fangs into Kat's willing, outstretched neck, the vampire leered at me and then hissed. It was Paw Paw.

I was running late the next morning when I joined Kat and Suzannah at the bus stop in front of the Barrington's house. Kat gave me a little wave and said "Hey" before turning away to continue chatting with Suzie about their teacher.

They were in the same homeroom class at Highlands Junior High.

"Oh, no," I cried, while thumbing through my stack of books. "I forgot my algebra workbook." I glanced at my psychedelic

Jackson Five wrist-watch. We had four minutes before the bus was due. "I'll be right back. Don't let the bus leave without me!"

I waited for some cars to zoom past, then hustled across the road and ran up our driveway, taking the kitchen steps two at a time. The workbook wasn't in my room—not on the coffee table in the den—wait—I remembered doing my math homework at the dining room table after supper, while everyone else was watching *Gunsmoke* in the den.

At the stove, Mama snapped, "You'd better hurry," and Daddy, who was off disability and back working full-time at the Winn-Dixie print shop by then, smiled over the top of the newspaper as I grabbed my workbook and sailed out the kitchen door onto the carport, just as I was sure I heard the bus squealing to a stop at the corner. *Drat.* I broke into a head-down run, arms pumping. I paused at the busy road, looking up. The bus wasn't there. *Weird.* I was sure I'd heard it. Had it already left?

I was halfway across when I saw a pair of tennis shoes lying in the middle of the intersection. A green and white PF Flyer logo shone in the morning sun. Somebody had thrown Kat's shoes into the road!

That's mean, I thought, and turned my head toward the corner, where my cousin stood with her arms folded around herself, as if suddenly cold. How had Suzie done such a thing, and why? Kat would pound her to dust.

I looked over toward where Suzie was staring.

Kat's clothes were lying in a heap on the side of the road— blue jeans, tee-shirt, white athletic socks.

Some man I didn't know jumped from the cab of a blue pickup truck, shouting, "I didn't see her! Sweet Jesus! I didn't see her!"

Ohmygoodness. Kat was in those clothes. She looked like a scarecrow, all straw and no bones.

Her sister Lucy burst out of the front door of their house. Her blonde hair was rolled up on orange juice cans. "SISSY!" she screamed. She covered her face with shaking hands tipped in bright pink nail polish.

A firm hand fell on my shoulder. "Step out of the street, Honey." Daddy walked me to the other side.

It made no sense, why Daddy moved so slowly, why Lucy stood and wept, why the man from the pickup truck repeated his strange litany. Someone should *hurry.*

Someone should *help* her. Someone should *fix this.*

Daddy sank to his knees in the dirt beside Kat. He laid two fingers on the side of her neck, put a flat palm to her chest, then gently closed her eyes. He took off his beat-up gray sweater, the one Mama kept threatening to throw out with the trash, and covered her face with it. Her lush auburn curls spilled out from underneath. Lucy crawled like a baby on hands and knees to grasp her sister's hand.

I watched all this and stood frozen, wondering why no one moved Kat's shoes out of the road.

Kat's arms, flung wide, brought flashing through my mind the prize-winning news photo still hanging on the wall of Jimmy's room, even though Suzie had moved in there a few weeks after he left home.

"No!" I yelled, and snatched the gray sweater from my friend's face, flinging it behind me. "You have to try the kiss of life. Please, Daddy."

He understood at once, and said to Lucy. "Go call an ambulance." Then he tilted Kat's head back, pinched her nose, and blew air into her mouth with his.

I dropped to my knees beside them, as Lucy ran back into her house to use the phone. "Doubt not," Saint Joan had said. "Work, and God will work also." Daddy labored beside me, pushing breath after breath into Kat's lungs. My job was to pray hard, and believe.

By the time the ambulance came, Kat was still unconscious, but breathing on her own. Mama stood by the side of the road, her arms wrapped around a pale and shaken Suzie. Kat's parents hovered, thunder-struck, watching the police talk to the man from the blue pickup truck, while Daddy sat, looking exhausted, in the dirt where he'd given Kat mouth-to-mouth.

Uncle Billy, Aunt Pat, and Lucy tore off in their Lincoln Continental, following the ambulance that raced Kat to the hospital, but not before Uncle Billy solemnly helped my daddy to his feet and shook his hand. They didn't say a word, but their welling eyes said it all. I'd never seen grown men cry before.

Before Kat got hit by that truck, death had always been a vague concept from a Sunday school lesson about Heaven, or something that happened to young men wearing uniforms in the jungles of Vietnam, or to old men in hospital cancer wards. Now it was a stark, undeniably real possibility for one of my friends. Kat clung to life at Memorial Hospital. If she woke up, she might not ever walk again. No one but her immediate family was allowed to see her.

Death could happen to kids like us. And not just in movies like *Billy Jack*, with the line Jimmy had liked to quote, "Today is as good a day as any to die."

Tragedy left its mark on Aunt Pat, Uncle Billy, and Lucy, who moved about with stunned faces, hunched deep within themselves, as if their bones were hollow and creaked when they walked. It left its mark on my cousin Suzannah, who hardly left the house except to go to church and school. She talked incessantly to her sisters on the party line, and held hands with one of us almost constantly, as if to keep safe through human contact.

Tragedy left its mark on my mama, who cried at the drop of a hat and shook her head and murmured about *that sweet, sweet child*, as if Kat had never done a thing wrong in her whole life.

It left its mark on my Daddy. Encountering such a young life almost snuffed out in an instant took all the pep out of him. He seemed to grow old overnight.

Tragedy left its mark on me. I felt Death hovering close. Whenever I closed my eyes, day or night, I saw Kat's shoes lying in the road.

One night I dreamed I heard her voice. "I'm not dead," she said.

"Yes, you really, really are," I answered.

In my nightmare, pallbearers carried a baby-blue-and-white coffin down the long aisle of Our Lady by the Sea and out the doors to a waiting hearse. Suzie stood on the church steps. "Holy Mackerel," she said. "Undertaker, take'er under."

I bit my knuckle so I wouldn't laugh—or scream. I woke, gasping.

Vengeance is MINE, Death whispered in the dark.

Thirteen

Despite our fears, Kat didn't die, and Lucy got used to popping over with updates on her condition. The Barringtons rightly considered Daddy to be their hero, but he was quick to point out that I'd reminded him to perform mouth-to-mouth. I knew at least part of the credit belonged to the Lord and Saint Joan. The three of us, we were a team. First we'd saved Daddy, now Kat. We probably could have saved Paw Paw, if I'd thought of it in time.

Kat wasn't allowed to have visitors besides her own family, but we celebrated each milestone with them as she woke up, then spoke a few words, began to feed herself, and finally got transferred to the Shriner's Hospital for Children in Tampa, where they hoped she'd eventually learn to walk again.

In August, a few months after the accident, Daddy rocked in his favorite chair in the den while Richard Milhouse Nixon gave a speech resigning as President of the United States.

"You're watching history, Honey," Mama said. "No other U.S. President has ever resigned before." Then she murmured, "I guess Jimmy was right. He was a crook."

"This country is going to Hell!" Daddy stood up so quickly, he sent his rocking chair skittering backward. He staggered toward the bathroom, where we heard him retching. Mama ran after him, while Suzie and I swapped disgusted glances.

"Gross," she said.

"Eww. Poor thing," I agreed. "He's really upset."

"Honey!" Mama shrieked. I raced around the corner, almost colliding with her as she ran back toward the den. Her body blocked my view of the bathroom, where Daddy knelt on the floor in front of the toilet, but not before I saw the bloody mess in the bowl and another on the floor beside it. I had never seen so much blood.

Mama grabbed my shoulders and spun me away from the sight. She gave me a push toward the living room.

"Call emergency," she ordered. "Tell them to come NOW."

She turned back to Daddy, shutting the bathroom door behind her.

I stood frozen, staring at the door. All that blood. How could he still be throwing up? How could he still be alive?

Suzie rounded the corner. "What's going on?" Her voice quavered.

Her words broke the spell and I sprang toward the phone. "I'm not sure." I snatched up the receiver. "Aunt Bonnie, Aunt Violet, hang up! Daddy's real sick—I need the line."

"James had a heart attack," said Dr. Holland. "I'm guessing the news about the President, on top of the death of your father, and the neighbor child's accident, was too much stress for him to handle."

"Will he be okay?" Mama wrung her hands.

"Hard to say. You called us quickly, and the rescue squad got him to the hospital fast. That's always best. But diabetes is hard on the heart, so we'll have to see how things go."

Doubt not. I heard the words of Joan of Arc in the back of my mind. This was another test of faith, that's all. Like when Abraham was told by an angel to take his son Isaac into the wilderness and sacrifice him on an altar to God. Abraham didn't doubt; he obeyed without question, and at the very last minute, God provided a ram to be the sacrifice, sparing Isaac's life.

I bowed my head at the foot of the hospital bed, and once more began to pray my father well. Before the week was out, we were able to take him home.

He didn't jog or ride his Honda anymore. He took another long leave of absence from work, and spent a lot of time in the rocking chair, reading his Bible, or recording his blood pressure in a little brown notebook. Sometimes he just sat, dangling his feet in the water off our dock on Bass River. He was pale and walked more slowly. But he was my Daddy, and he was alive, and that was enough for me.

He'd been home from the hospital for about a week when I saw Daddy's notebook lying on the coffee table by his rocking chair. Alone in the room and feeling curious, I opened it at random. What was he always scribbling in there?

Went to see Brother D. today at the church, to ask why God hasn't healed me yet, but he was busy counseling someone else, so I left. So many questions; no answers.

I don't know what to do. So hard to see my family do things I used to do for them.

I was shocked. Was Daddy afraid? Reading his secret thoughts felt worse than if I'd seen him naked.

I guess he knew the power of the number three, as well as I did. Across the bottom of the page were written these words:

Help. Help. Help!

Part Four

1975

Fourteen

Daddy had always had a great sense of humor. He loved to pull jokes on people while keeping a perfectly straight face. He could tell the biggest whopping lies with such a serious, sincere expression that his gullible victims wanted to believe him, and the rest of us in the family, who knew he was telling a tall tale, would finally have pity on them and burst out laughing, giving him away and ruining his fun.

But as his diabetes worsened, he could be impatient, even mean. Like one morning when I was fifteen.

It was St. Patrick's Day, and I planned to wear a kelly green pullover and bell-bottomed jeans, along with an emerald shamrock necklace my mother had given me the night before. I was scared if I didn't wear green on St. Patrick's Day, the kids at school would pinch me.

Before I could dress like a leprechaun, I needed a shower. I stepped from my bedroom into the hall, and was nearly run down by Doodle the Poodle. He skittered around me, toenails snarling the carpet for traction.

Our bathroom, hall closets, and kitchen pantry formed the center of our house, with all the other rooms radiating out from them in a circle. It was an odd arrangement, but cozy, and one that Doodle loved because he could race around and around the circle seven, eight, nine times at full speed before collapsing in exhausted exhilaration on the rug in the den. I watched the curly little dog in amazement at times like that, wondering what inner voice told him to start running, how he managed to go at such a break-neck pace and not hit anything like a wall or a chair or a human foot, and why he suddenly, just as inexplicably, stopped.

Like Doodle, only slower, we walked the circle countless times every day, moving from kitchen to dining room to living room, past first my parent's bedroom, then mine, then Suzie's (although to me, it would always be Jimmy's), through the den, and back to the kitchen. The single bathroom the four of us shared was across from my bedroom, so of course there were many trips in and out of there every day, to bathe, to use the toilet, to brush our teeth and wash our hands, and for me to check the medicine chest's mirror for a new batch of pimples to coat with Noxema.

After taking a shower, I dressed hurriedly in the bathroom and wrapped my wet hair in a towel. I walked down the hallway to the den, stopping on the way to drop my pajamas into the dirty-clothes hamper beside the bathroom door. Daddy sat in his Boston rocker in the den. He faced the television set, but had his Bible open on his knee. He leaned over, scratching Doodle behind the ears. The dog's tongue was hanging out, and his eyes were closed, as if being scratched in this way was what life was all about.

I swooped down to give my father a kiss on the cheek, and Doodle a pat on his fat little belly.

"Morning, Daddy," I said.

"Morning, Honey-bun."

He wore his light blue pajamas trimmed with white piping, and a plaid flannel bathrobe. He smelled faintly like yesterday's

Aqua Velva aftershave, which I loved, and I lingered for a moment. I liked the way the morning stubble on his cheek felt against my own smooth one, so I gave him a hug, bending over to lay my face against his as he straightened in the rocking chair. He was almost perfectly bald on top now, with only remnants of salt and pepper hair on the sides of his head.

I glanced at the television. Daddy was watching a meteorologist give the weather report on Channel Four. My father kept up with the weather, because he still loved to fish. Even then, when he could no longer go to his job at the Winn-Dixie print shop because his doctor had him on extended sick leave, he would make his way down our hill to the dock and sit there for hours with a cane pole.

I crossed in front of the television and made my way into the kitchen. Half of the wall between the kitchen and the den was a cutout pass-through, so conversation was still easy.

"Have you had breakfast, Daddy?"

"I'm not hungry."

I walked to the doorway, put my hand on my hip, and gave him a look that would have made Mama proud if she hadn't been helping Suzie find a green satin scarf to tie around her pony tail.

"Cereal or eggs?"

He sighed. "You can make me some toast."

Still watching TV, Daddy played "My Bonnie Lies Over the Ocean" on the harmonica as I went back into the kitchen and put two slices of bread into the toaster. While they toasted, I walked back through the den to my bedroom, where I unwrapped my wet hair, gave it a quick fluff with the towel, and combed it out with my wide-toothed comb so it wouldn't snarl. I blew a kiss to Elvis Presley's photo, which was stuck in the frame of my dresser's mirror, and blew another kiss to my poster of David Cassidy, which hung on my bedroom door. I imagined the two of them fighting over me, and smiled.

Suzannah asked if she could borrow a plastic shamrock ring I'd gotten in a box of Cracker Jacks, and I said, "Sure."

"Honey," my father called, "my toast is getting cold."

I hurried down the hall and around the corner and passed between him and the television again. "Sorry, Daddy." This time he didn't say anything to me, just leaned to one side to better see the television around me. An anchorman was reading the morning news.

I spread the toast with butter substitute and sugar-free grape jelly and took it to Daddy on a plate. He moved the Bible from his knee to the coffee table, and set the plate with the toast on his lap.

I crossed in front of the television again and returned to the kitchen, where I poured myself a bowl of Cap'n Crunch and ate it at the kitchen table. Suzie joined me for a bowl of her own. I read the book reviews and the comics from the *Florida Times-Union* while I ate my breakfast.

Suzie murmured about something one of her sisters had said on the phone the night before. The television news droned on in the den, and I could hear the rushing water of my mother taking her shower in the bathroom.

After I finished my cereal, I washed the bowl and spoon and placed them in the dish drainer to air-dry. I heard the bathroom door open, meaning Mama was finished with her shower, and I could brush my teeth before catching the school bus.

I started to cross between my father and the television again. He'd had it.

"Why don't you think of a hundred more reasons to walk back and forth in front of the TV, okay? I'm not trying to watch it or anything."

I slammed on the brakes instantly, my back up, sarcasm at the ready. I bowed like a courtier before a king, my imaginary feathered hat sweeping the carpet in front of the television.

"Excuse me!" I muttered, under my breath. I could have kept going forward out of the room. Instead, I backed up slowly, doing an exaggerated tiptoe through the kitchen, and around our house the other way.

I stomped into the bathroom, closing the door with a resounding slam. I slathered my toothbrush with Crest and scowled into the mirror as I brushed my teeth. My parents never appreciated anything! I saw the anger in my eyes evaporate into fear when I heard my father call from the den.

"Help me."

He didn't shout; it was more of a whimper, but it brought my mother, my cousin and me to the den at a run. Mama took one look at Daddy and said, "Honey, call emergency."

Daddy stood from the rocking chair and, leaning on my mother, walked slowly across the den and down the hall to their bedroom. She was dressed for work in a pink polyester dress with a pleated skirt, so they made an odd pair as he shuffled beside her in his robe and slippers. Suzie stood by the rocking chair with wide eyes and hugged herself in her usual self-comforting gesture. I could hear the creak of the springs as Daddy sank onto his bed, even as I moved quickly into our dining room and dialed the emergency number.

I experienced an eerie déjà vu. On one level, I gave the dispatcher the information she requested: my name, the nature of the problem, our address, our telephone number, my father's name. On another level, I heard the alarm bell ringing at the fire station, watched the paramedics clamber into the white ambulance van. "Come quickly," I urged.

Then I called on my own, personal rescue squad.

Help us, Jesus, Help us, Saint Joan, I prayed. *Help my Daddy.*

I hung up the phone and walked from the dining room, through the living room, into my parents' bedroom. My mother stood with her back to the door, snatching things my father would need at the hospital from the bureau drawers. He lay on top of the white chenille spread on their double bed with his eyes closed and one hand on his chest. With the other hand, he clutched a throw pillow like a lifeline. I sat on the bed beside him, and he opened his eyes to look at me. They were bloodshot and full of fear. I stared into them, needing him to hear and understand me; needing more than anything to apologize.

"Sorry, Daddy. You're going to be okay. I love you."

"Luyu," he said.

We heard the wail of approaching sirens.

"Go stand in the driveway and wave them in, Baby," said Mama.

I squeezed Daddy's hand and brushed past Suzie, who watched from the bedroom doorway.

The paramedics knew our family and we knew them by name. Although they maintained their professional demeanor, their caring showed. I grabbed my purse, my Bible, and my thick white button-up sweater on our way out of the house.

"Can I ride with Daddy?" I asked. Mama looked at John, the paramedic in charge, who nodded.

"I'll bring the car," Mama said. She turned to my cousin, who once again stood motionless, all big eyes. "Grab your jacket and come with me, Suzie."

After the medics loaded Daddy into the back of the ambulance, I jumped into the front seat with the driver while Mama and Suzie followed in the Green Hornet.

Jacksonville Memorial Hospital was in Arlington, across the St. John's River from our Northside home. As we navigated through the traffic and across the bridge, I "prayed without ceasing." As Southern Baptists, we didn't believe in the need for an intercessor like a priest or a saint when we wanted to talk to God. But Saint Joan was different. She was my hero, and part of the miracle team.

I considered the members of the Holy Trinity to be somewhat interchangeable, although there was a certain ratcheting-up of respect when I spoke to God, a certain friendliness when I spoke to Jesus, and I only talked to the Holy Spirit on those rare occasions when I felt blissful and full and anointed, usually during a revival at church, or when Brother Dimmesdale sang "In the Garden."

That day, as the ambulance driver kept in contact with the paramedics who were caring for my father in the back of the van, and with the emergency room staff awaiting our arrival at the hospital, it was my friend, Jesus, I talked to while I struggled to keep my balance on the slippery vinyl front seat. We weaved in and out of traffic much faster than I'd ever ridden, with lights and siren blaring.

Lord, please forgive me for being a smart-aleck to Daddy. Saint Joan, please help us as we fight this battle.

When we arrived at the emergency room, the paramedics rushed my father through the double swinging doors and my mother and cousin hurried in right behind us.

"Dr. Holland is on staff. Please let him know James Lee is here," said Mama to the lady at the admissions desk.

The clerk checked her clip-board. "Dr. Holland is at the TPC." I knew she meant the Tournament Players Championship, a prestigious golf tournament being played at nearby Ponte Vedra Beach. Overhearing this, I imagined Dr. Holland (whom I liked because he exuded quiet competence from a tall, gangly frame) ambling along the fairway behind the famous golfers he admired, soaking up the beautiful Florida sunshine, never guessing that my father, one of his favorite patients, was struggling for life only minutes away. "Don't worry," the clerk reassured my mother, patting her arm, "We have some very fine doctors on call today. Your husband is in good hands."

I looked at my mother, whisper-thin and nervous, hoping she wouldn't cause a fuss. Mama would give you the shirt off her back, but you didn't want to cross her. I could well imagine her making a scene, insisting Dr. Holland be summoned at once.

Just then, we heard loud, urgent voices on the other side of the swinging doors where they had taken my father. They were shouting at him.

"C'mon, Mr. Lee! Stay with us! You've got to fight, James!"

My breath, my heart, my mind, froze. This could not be happening. It felt like an episode of the TV show, *Emergency*, except it was my father's life on the line, not some actor's. The lights over our heads seemed too bright; voices too loud. I could smell rubbing alcohol, urine, Lysol, and blood.

Fifteen

It could not be happening, but it was. Mama's lovely ice blue eyes widened. I could feel her panic rising. She squeezed my hand so hard I had to pull away before she crushed my fingers. I felt helpless.

"He's going, he's going," Mama said.

"Let's pray, Mama," I patted her hand with my throbbing fingertips. The admissions clerk waited in her chair behind the desk, giving us time.

"Lord," my mother whispered, "please save my husband." Her face dissolved into tears.

"Lord," I said, a little louder, "Please help my daddy."

You, too, Saint Joan.

"Amen," intoned Suzannah.

"Amen," said the admissions clerk, her eyes shining. She gave our family a moment, and then asked in a gentle tone for more information about Daddy.

Mama finished the paperwork and called JC Penney's to tell her boss why she wouldn't be at work that day. She settled into a hard, plastic waiting room chair after she called the school to tell them Suzie and I wouldn't be at school, either. Suzie and I flanked my mother, trying to give her strength. Mostly, we prayed.

We all looked up sometime later at the whoosh of the emergency room doors. I realized I was waiting for Jimmy to walk in and scan the room. I would be happy to have someone else to hold Mama's death grip hand for a while. Her fear, her neediness, drained me. My brother was short, like Daddy, but quite good-looking with his wispy dark brown hair brushing the shoulders of his stylish CPO jacket. He was my mother's favorite, although she would deny she had a favorite, if you asked her. But I knew better. He and Mama had always been close. She felt he needed her more than I, the independent one, did. What she didn't know was that I had my needy times, too. I'd just always turned to prayer when I felt that way. I'd talk to Jesus, seek his answers in the pages of my New Testament, and feel confident that I could face whatever needed facing. Between my brother having to hide away or be sent to die in Vietnam and caring for my father and her niece, Mama had enough troubles.

Anyway, I knew I was Daddy's girl.

A young man who resembled, but wasn't, Jimmy crossed the waiting room and sat on a table, scattered with outdated magazines, talking to an old man in a chair. His jeans were stained, as were his beige desert boots.

"I don't know how to get hold of your brother," Mama said, so I knew she'd noticed the resemblance, too.

I tried to distract her. "What do you think is wrong with Daddy?" I asked Mama.

She teared up again and reached for my hand. "I think it's another stroke ... a bad one."

Just then the double doors my father had disappeared behind popped open and a man in green hospital scrubs and a paper cap approached us. He looked too young to be a doctor but the name tag pinned to his chest assured us he was. He carried a clipboard, and his eyes were very tired. I stared at the blood flecks on his shirt. Did he know they were there?

"Are you James Lee's family?" We nodded three heads as one. "I'm Dr. Peronto. Mr. Lee is having a rough time right now. Can you come with me, please?"

We rose together and followed him through the swinging doors. He led us past the rows of treatment rooms, most with pastel-striped curtains partially drawn, revealing patients in various states of ill health and undress. I felt embarrassed for them as I glanced into each one, knowing I was invading their privacy, but frustrated, too, because I wanted to see my father. No dice. The doctor ushered us into a small room with a round table and some chairs. The three of us sat, but Dr. Peronto leaned against the wall and rubbed his eyes. He sighed, then gathered himself and began.

"We're fairly certain that James has suffered a cerebral hemorrhage. This is similar to a stroke, but on a massive scale. We've given him medication to control the bleeding, but he's in bad shape." The doctor touched the tips of his fingers with his thumb, ticking off the details of my daddy's condition. "He's having trouble breathing, so we've put him on a respirator. We know he's had a history of heart attack, so we've attached a machine to monitor and regulate that, too."

"He'll be all right, won't he?" my mother asked.

"There is always a possibility of damage to the brain from bleeding like this. We need to do some tests, specifically an electroencephalogram, or EEG, to check on his brain functions. I'll need you to sign some papers giving us permission."

"Anything you need," Mama said.

He handed her the clipboard with a sheaf of papers, all of which my mother signed. She barely glanced at any of them.

Suzie spoke up, asking a grown-up question that I should have asked. "When can we see him?"

I listened, feeling small and left out.

"He's being moved to intensive care," said the doctor. "It's the best place to monitor everything we need to evaluate at this time, help him breathe, keep his heart rate steady. Once we've got him stabilized, you can see him. Visitation in ICU is every four hours, around the clock. But we ask that you see him one at a time, for only five minutes each."

He let that news sink in. Then he suggested we take the next hour to get a bite to eat, and he walked us to a long corridor, pointing the way to the hospital cafeteria.

"We know the way," said Suzie.

That's where we were, over an hour later, when Dr. Holland, my father's personal physician, found us. He was dressed casually, having dropped by the hospital to check on his patients on his way home from the golf tournament. His skin was burnt from walking in the sun all morning, and his black hair was tousled from the wind. At the bottom cuff of his trousers there were beggar's lice, sticky little seeds from Y-shaped plants that must have hitched a ride after he walked through the high grass in the rough, following the golfers. He greeted my mother with affection and smiled at my cousin and me.

"Lord, Rose, I wish I had been here. I never would have let this happen," he said.

"You couldn't have prevented it, Dr. Holland," Mama said. "He had the hemorrhage at home."

"I meant the life support." His voice was soft. He took my mother's hand in both of his across the cafeteria table.

"The EEG was flat, Rose. No brain activity. What that means is that, technically, James has passed on. I knew how sick he was, with the previous stroke and the heart attack. He might only be forty-three, but he has the circulatory system of an eighty-year-old man. I'd warned you that this time was coming, sooner than we'd like. I would have let it happen, naturally, because it was time."

The noise of the cafeteria with its plastic, clacking trays faded as the room spun. I gripped the table and tried to focus on what the doctor was saying. Did he mean that my father was dead? That Mama knew he was dying?

Lord Jesus, I prayed. Just his name.

"The emergency room doctors did what they were trained to do," Dr. Holland said. "They tried to save his life, using whatever means they had. You signed papers to put him on life support. Do you understand what I'm telling you?"

I looked at the stricken faces of my mother and cousin, and knew that a thousand questions with no answers were flying through their brains, just like mine.

Mama shook her head.

The doctor continued, "There is a legal process this hospital must go through before it can take a patient off life-support machines. We have to have five perfectly flat brain scans, which would indicate zero brain activity. And the scans have to be taken twenty-four hours apart."

"You've taken the first one?" my mother asked.

"Yes."

"And it was flat?"

"Yes," he repeated.

No one spoke for a moment. Suzie looked as if she wished she was back at the Baptist Home for Children. Sometimes being an almost-orphan was easier.

"Is it possible Uncle James is just in a coma?" Suzie asked.

"That's what the brain scans will tell us. That's why we have to be careful."

I latched onto the word "coma" like a drowning child.

That was it. Daddy was resting. He was in a deep, deep sleep. He was gathering his strength, and when he was ready, he would come back to me. To us.

I stood, scraping my chair across the cafeteria's tile floor. "I'm going for a walk." Nobody stopped me.

I knew the way to the chapel without looking at the signs. Down the hall, past the gift shop, across from the elevators closest to the lobby. Once there, I whispered my secrets to Jesus. I confessed that Daddy was in intensive care because of me. As I prayed, I trembled.

He's only forty-three years old, Lord, but he's had diabetes since he was fourteen. He's been pretty sick for the past few years, but I know the cerebral hemorrhage is my doing. I'm the one who made him mad this morning.

This is all my fault. Don't punish him; punish me.

I liked the chapel's quiet coolness. It was a fine place to think. I had spent time there before, praying my father through his illnesses. That was one of the other secrets I shared with Jesus that day. I reminded him of the times we'd worked together to pull my Daddy through, and to save Kat's life. I kept it a secret because I knew folks would think it was a sin, me taking credit for partnering with Jesus. But it took two; Him to work the miracle, and me to have faith the size of a mustard seed. Without my faith, no miracle. With Saint Joan thrown in, we were the Three Musketeers, an unstoppable trinity.

During the prior couple of years, Dr. Holland had warned us that the side effects of stroke might include paralysis and speech impediments. Daddy's left hand and arm were weak for a while, and his voice slurred a little, but I prayed and read my Bible and believed, and he'd recovered the use of his limbs, and his speech was clear.

I felt special, singled out. I didn't hear voices or see visions, as Joan of Arc did, and I was certainly no saint, as Suzannah and Kat would have testified, but Jesus spoke to me from the pages of my Bible. Like Saint Joan, I was a child warrior. Her battlegrounds were the blood-soaked fields of France; mine were the halls of Jacksonville Memorial Hospital. She fought to save her country; I battled to save my Daddy.

I got him into this mess with my sassing. Together, Jesus and I could get him out.

I bowed my head in the chapel and prayed again.

Lord, Dr. Holland says my Daddy might be dead, but I know something the doctors don't know. Mama and Suzie don't know it, either. I have faith the size of a mustard seed, and nothing is impossible for me. Because nothing is impossible for You.

I don't care what those brain scans say.

I don't care what the doctors say.

I know this is a test of faith, and I know that we can make my Daddy well. We've done it before. They thought Kat was dead, and we brought her back to life. I know You won't let me down, Lord, because You never, ever have.

Thank you, Jesus. Thank you, God. Thank you, Saint Joan.

I made the sign of the cross three times. *Amen.*

I lifted my head. The copper taste of fear had turned to steel somewhere deep inside me. When I left the chapel to go find my mother and cousin, to visit my father in ICU, I was no longer afraid. Jesus, Saint Joan and I had a deal. No matter what the doctors or anyone else thought, I believed.

Sixteen

For the next five days, we lived in the intensive care unit waiting room. We slept on cramped, uncomfortable chairs pulled together to make little nests. I covered myself with my white sweater, Suzie with one of Jimmy's old CPO jackets, my mother with her linen coat. Suzie and I nestled like puppies, wrapped around each other for warmth and comfort. We ate meals in the hospital cafeteria, when we remembered to eat at all.

The intensive care unit didn't have separate rooms in those days. It was just a huge space with beds placed in a loose semi-circle. Each bed held a critically ill patient surrounded by various beeping, buzzing, wheezing machines. The patients were draped with intravenous and breathing tubes. I imagined that each bore very little resemblance to the person they had been on the outside of the hospital. The same pastel-striped curtains that provided paltry privacy in the emergency room hung between the beds to mark the borders of each patient's tiny space.

From time to time, between visits to Daddy's bedside, one or the other of our aunts drove us girls home to tend to Doodle, take a shower, and pick up clean clothes for Mama. Her hair grew oily and lank, but she wouldn't go home long enough to shower; she made do with a "bird-bath" in the hospital ladies' room in the wee hours of the morning, when no one was likely to come in and catch her.

School and jobs and life in general seemed distant and unimportant. Mama selling bracelets to bored housewives at Penney's and Suzie and me doing homework suddenly seemed trivial. Time did not move in an ordinary fashion. It stood stark still for long periods, and then several hours passed without notice. Visitors from church and school came and went. They had the same sad faces, mouthed the same useless clichés about God's will and modern medical miracles. They meant well, and it cheered us briefly to see them, even if they couldn't visit Daddy in ICU, but scans two, three and four came back the same: flatline.

After each day's negative result, my mind skidded over what-if's. *No!* I told myself. That was the Devil talking. *Get behind me, Satan.*

When I wasn't eating or sleeping or reading outdated magazines, trying not to think, I prayed. I asked God hundreds of times a day for a miracle, reminded Jesus of our deal, and begged Saint Joan to help me until sweat popped out on my forehead. I needed to pray that final brain scan into frantic activity. *Doubt not*, I reminded myself.

So it wasn't surprising that I was in the chapel, praying for just one blip on the fifth scan, when Dr. Holland brought my mother and cousin the final results.

When I walked back into the intensivecare waiting room, most of my aunts and uncles were there. I didn't like the looks on their faces when they glanced up and saw me, or the shattered silhouettes of Mama and Suzie, who had both been crying, hard. I turned on my heels and bolted for the ladies' room.

I was sitting in a toilet stall when the bathroom door slowly opened. I could tell from the footfalls that it was my mother. *Not yet, not yet, not yet* was all I could think.

Stop that. Doubt not.

"Honey?" My mother's voice was brittle. In that one word, I could hear how close she was to the breaking point.

I had to be brave, like Saint Joan. Face the fire. My mother needed me.

I had to believe. My father needed me.

I opened the stall door, walked to the sink, and began washing my hands, not looking at my mother.

"Baby, they've done the final brain scan. There was nothing."

I dried my hands, throwing the wet, crumpled towel into the trash basket.

No, that can't be. We have a deal.

"Dr. Holland is going to disconnect the life-support machines in a little while. We've been waiting for you, so that you can say your good-byes."

I stared at the floor. How could she ask me to do that?

How could I tell him good-bye?

I felt as if Daddy's life rested in my fifteen-year-old hands. I pictured him, healthy, mullet net draped over his arm, and I could swear I smelled Vidalia onions.

"Let's pray, Mama. God will give us a miracle."

Mama's voice broke as she struggled not to cry. "Don't you think I'd be down on my knees, right here, right now, if I thought there was a chance? The doctor says the time for miracles is past, Baby. There's nothing more they can do. He says we have to let your Daddy go now." She looked crushed by the weight of her words, like a puff of air or a drop of rain would dissolve her.

I didn't want to believe her. Yet how could I not?

Science had done all it could do.

I finally looked at my mother. She didn't know. Dr Holland didn't know. Only Jesus, Saint Joan, and I knew about the deal. I reached out and took Mama's hand. "Okay," I said.

"I'm so sorry," Mama said. Then she sobbed so hard her knees buckled.

I held her up and cried, too, hugging her as tight as I could, burying my head into the soft curve where her neck met her shoulder. I wanted to stay there and be her little girl, safe and secure. But I knew that if what she'd said was true, I would never feel like a child again.

"It will be all right, Mama," I said. I felt surrounded by a bubble of white light, as if the Holy Spirit was holding me in His arms.

When we walked out of the bathroom, Suzie was leaning against the wall beside the door. They walked with me to the ICU. Suzie put one arm around my waist and held onto my mother with the other. Mama froze at the curtain that partitioned Daddy's room from the others. "I can't go in there again."

Mama looked ready to collapse, so I told Suzie, "Take her back to the waiting room. I'll be okay."

I parted the curtain and walked to my father's side. I knew how Shadrach, Meshach and Abednego must have felt in the fiery furnace.

Daddy's right hand lay on his chest. It looked natural lying there, as if he was just asleep. He was covered by a thin white blanket, and I watched his hand rise and fall, rise and fall, as the respirator breathed for him through the tube snaking in the right side of his mouth. The bump-bump of the heart machine was steady and strong. I looked at his sweet, sleeping face, stared at his wisps of salt-and-pepper hair. I remembered his boisterous laugh. They had told me the time for praying for a miracle was past, but I knew better. I took his big, warm left hand and held it with my small one.

"I love you, Daddy. Wake up."

I thought about what would happen if they unhooked the machines, if they no longer forced his heart to beat, his lungs to rise and fall. Would he struggle for air? Would it hurt? What if they made this horrible mistake?

Daddy's hand moved across his chest, down his body, and came to rest on the bed beside his leg. My eyes grew wide; my breath caught. I knew it! My prayers were answered. *Thank you, Jesus.* God had given me a miracle!

I don't remember shouting, though I must have, because the duty nurse came bounding over. Her alert green eyes swept around the room, taking in the monitors, my father's face, and me, all at once.

"He moved! He moved his arm!" I wept. God had kept his promise. My father was alive!

But something was wrong.

The nurse gathered me in her arms. "Hush, baby, hush," she crooned. "It's just a muscle spasm. It happens with people on life support. Your daddy's gone."

No! He couldn't be. Why would she say such a terrible thing? Couldn't she see it was a miracle?

I searched her eyes, frantic. Truth and compassion were all I saw.

I turned toward my father, lying still once more.

Reality settled over me like a shroud. The nurse was right. He wasn't there.

There would be no miracle.

Everything I'd ever believed unraveled, like a giant spool of black thread lying tangled on the floor at my feet. Science had spoken. God remained silent.

I pushed the nurse away and ran from the room.

Seventeen

Mama handed over her credit card and agreed that she would stay home with Suzie to rest. Maw Maw would take me to make arrangements for Daddy at the funeral parlor that had handled everything when Paw Paw died.

"They show you the expensive stuff first, so the trick is to always order from the middle third of the list," Maw Maw said, once we were about to go inside. "Anything lower than that is cheap junk you wouldn't lay your dog to rest in, and anything higher is just wasting a widow's money."

I felt fury that Daddy would have to settle for anything less than the best. He'd had life insurance through Winn-Dixie, after all. Then again, Mama and I would need most of that money to live on, so I had to admit Maw Maw was right.

We were frugal enough, picking out the gravesite, the casket, and the vault ... right up until the funeral director showed us the photos of the flowers for the top of the casket. I thought of my father's love of the floral still lifes at the Cummer Museum, and his delight when Kat'd found the dewdrop on the petal of the rose. I remembered him strolling with my mother in her garden, inhaling the fragrance of her flowers. I pointed to the very first, most expensive picture in the book. "We'll take that one." If it took our last or only penny, my father's final blanket would be red roses, greenery, and baby's breath, from the top of his head to the soles of his feet.

After the burial, folks came back to our house with enough food and drink to last for weeks. It was the Southern way. Mama took one of the nerve pills from the sample bottle Dr. Holland had given her and lay down on the bed without eating, with Suzie sitting beside her, holding her hand.

They left me to play hostess. I chatted, I smiled, I poured a river of iced tea and hot coffee.

Maw Maw took charge in the kitchen, making sure folks had what they needed, wrapping things for the freezer, refilling plates each time they emptied. As if enough food would make everything better. I ate three big plates of ham with macaroni and cheese.

When the last guest had left, I went into the bathroom and threw it all up.

Within the week, before we even went back to work and school, our telephone rang for the millionth time. Mama picked up the receiver in the living room, shooing me away with her free hand, saying, "Hello, Brother," into the phone. That phony-baloney Uncle Travis hadn't made it to his own brother in law's funeral. Why was he pestering us now? Suzannah was taking a nap in her bedroom, out of ear-shot, and I thought about picking up the extension in the den, but wasn't brave enough. Instead, I lingered by the bookcase in the hall, where I could hear Mama's end of the conversation, yet pretend to be choosing a book if I got caught listening.

The two adults had a long, serious talk. It was the first time I'd heard Mama stir from her zombie-like state, though her voice still sounded monotone. I blamed the nerve pills for her sleepiness, but she seemed to crave them, and got shrill and shaky when it was time for another dose.

"I'm proud of you for going to AA," I heard Mama say. "A whole year sober, huh?" I doubted Uncle Travis could make it a week without drinking, much less a year. Of course, I doubted almost everything after Daddy died.

She was quiet for a while, listening, and then Mama asked, "When did she come back home?" She waited. "What kind of medication is she on?" I figured out she meant Aunt Rita Faye, and I got a funny feeling in the pit of my stomach.

Mama murmured some things I couldn't hear, then, "Oh, no. I couldn't part with that. Would you like a few of his ties?"

She listened some more, then Mama said, quite perky, "Oh, Brother! I'm so glad you got saved!" I snorted, unable to even imagine Uncle Travis in church. Not that it mattered. Church, I now believed, was just a place to sing songs and hear stories.

Mama listened for a little while longer and then said, "I'll talk to the girls and call you back."

I knew it was serious when she woke Suzie from her nap and called us into the front living room. Most of the time we gathered in the den.

Suzie rubbed the sleep from her eyes.

"Your daddy wants to get your family back together." Suzie stared at Mama. "All of you. Your mama, your sisters, Little Travis, and you. Not for a visit. For good."

"You said 'No,' right, Mama?" I asked. Suzie'd lived with us for four years, and now Uncle Travis wanted to take her away!

Mama looked at me. There was a hitch in her breathing I'd never heard before.

"It's up to Suzie and her sisters," she said. Her voice reminded me of the robot-man in Paw Paw's hospital room, as if she was too tired to make a choice, like her give-a-dang was busted.

It took Suzie all of three seconds to decide.

She looked at me and grinned. Her black eyes danced as she nodded at Mama, then reached out and squeezed her hand. "I really like it here, but I reckon I'd better go home with my mama and daddy," Suzie said, like she'd been expecting this news every minute of every day. I was sure she had.

The old jealousy slammed hard into my chest. Suzie's faith in her family had been rewarded. Even God liked her best.

Mama's left eye twitched, but her expression never changed. She just stood up and went to her room to lie down.

Suzie called her father, then each of her sisters, on the party line, chattering with excitement.—*We get to see Mom. We'll have a new school. I hope we get our own closets.*—then she got up, went into her bedroom, and started stuffing her meager belongings into plastic garbage bags; she still had no luggage. I followed her, sat on the bed, and watched.

I didn't blame her for wanting to leave our house of sadness. Everyone was gone—Daddy, Jimmy, Paw Paw and Kat. Now it was Suzie's turn. But how would I handle Mama without her?

She would leave in the morning. For once, I had nothing to say.

The time on my clock radio glowed 3:24 a.m. when Suzie shook me awake. It was too dark to see her face clearly, but her silhouette spoke earnestly. "Honey, I know it's a bad time to be leaving you and Aunt Rose. I'll stay if you think y'all need me."

Hope rose in my chest; I wanted to tell her *yes, stay.* Who knew how safe or happy she'd be with her parents?

And who knew whether I could help Mama through the Valley of the Shadow alone?

But she'd waited half her life to have the chance to live a normal life with her own family. How could I ask her to stay?

"Don't be silly, Suz," I said. "Don't you dare spend another second worried about us. We'll be fine."

She was asleep again within minutes. I stared at the wall and worried enough through the long night for all of us.

Uncle Travis wasted no time getting to our house the next day. He was driving a decent-enough car. The way he sauntered up our driveway made me wish I had Daddy's pistol handy, so I could shoot the grin right off his face.

Mama'd said at breakfast that Travis had asked about Daddy's harmonica when he'd called her on the phone about fetching Suzie, wanting to know if he might have it to remember Daddy by. Mama had offered him some neckties instead, but he'd claimed he had plenty of those. There was no way I'd invite him into the house today, to paw through Daddy's things.

I moved fast, dashing from the clothesline where I'd been hanging towels to the carport, where I snatched up the broom that leaned against the wall between the steps and the washing machine. I slashed it left and right, scattering hickory nuts and oak leaves into Mama's flower beds. I thought about cracking him on the head with the broom or with one of the hickory nuts, which made even better projectiles than rocks. I remembered having bruises from Jimmy's perfect aim to prove it.

Though I only saw him from the corner of my eye, he looked better than I remembered. He wore a nicely pressed suit, and his face had lost that reddish tinge that used to tell us when he'd been drinking, which was almost all the time. He favored Mama, but though he was two years younger than her, the effects of hard living made him look much older than thirty-six.

I wouldn't say hello to him and I wouldn't look him in the eye. That would imply respect, and I was too furious for that. I nodded tersely at his greeting and kept on sweeping.

"Your mama home, gal?" he asked.

He knew she was; he'd set up this time to come and get Suzie. Mama could barely get out of bed from grief, and here he was to add to it by taking her favorite niece away. I couldn't stop him from picking up his daughter, though it just might kill Mama to lose her, but he could forget it if he'd come to torment my mother further by trying to get some of Daddy's belongings.

Something about the way Uncle Travis looked at me was scary, and then I realized what it was. He resembled his father physically, the way many sons do, but the way he resembled Paw Paw the most was in his attitude toward females. Charm them, use them, beat them, throw them away, take them back, kill them. It was all the same—females were a man's property, to do with as he saw fit.

The hairs on the back of my neck stood up.

Uncle Travis sat down on the steps with a sigh, like he was settling in for a visit. At least I could try to keep him outside, away from Mama.

"You still managing the 7-Eleven?" I asked. He grunted a yes.

I thought fast. "How's Little Travis?"

His face lit up, and eager words of praise for his one and only son tumbled out of his mouth. I didn't listen to what he said. It was just noise that droned on for a while.

I leaned on the broom for a moment, while Uncle Travis stood up and brushed off the seat of his pants.

Bragging on Little Travis seemed to satisfy whatever itch had caused him to want to chat with me.

"Tell your Mama I'm here," he said. "Tell her I've come to get Suzie, and to find out if y'all need anything."

I'll take care of Mama. We don't need anything from the likes of you, I thought.

"Yessir." I flourished the broom in a little wave, instead of giving him the hug I would have had to give him if Mama had been outside.

"Tell Suzie I'm in a hurry. I'll get the car started." Halfway to his car, he turned back, as if he'd only just then remembered something else. "Hey, what's your mama gonna do with your Daddy's cast nets?"

Cold fury gripped my heart. Heat blazed from my eyes. So there it was. I looked straight at him and lied like Satan. "She's saving them for Jimmy. Daddy wanted him to have them when he comes back home, after the war's over."

Before I went to fetch my cousin, I finished sweeping the carport, just because he had told me to hurry. Left, right. Swish, slash.

Sooner than I could go inside, I saw Suzannah hovering at the window. She spotted Uncle Travis's car and flew out of the house, banging the screen door behind her in a way that would have put Mama in a snit any other time. That day Mama managed one of her robot smiles and ambled over with the few pitiful garbage bags that held my cousin's belongings. She even gave Uncle Travis a hug and a kiss on the cheek.

"Hello, Brother," she said. Her smile was warm, but I knew that, even in her zombie-state, she was smelling his breath, making sure, before she'd let her little chick ride in the car with him. What an actress she could be when the situation called for it. Old habits, learned from being Paw Paw's child, died hard.

Mama took Uncle Travis's hand. "Y'all call us if y'all need anything, hear?" she said.

Yeah, I thought, like somebody to pick you up out of the gutter when you fall off the wagon again, you old . . . you old . . . but I didn't know a word bad enough for how I felt about him. Even Maw Maw's cuss words fell short of the mark. Was I the only one who remembered all the times he'd promised to straighten up and fly right, only to ruin a family gathering with his drunken rage? Was I the only one who recalled the times he'd picked up his girls from the Home, only to ship them right back again? I knew I should try to forgive, like Jesus said, but I'd always been lousy at forgetting. Plus, since Jesus hadn't listened to me, why should I listen to Him?

Suzie threw her arms around my neck. I hugged and kissed her.

"I'll miss you, Honey. Call me!" she said.

"Be good, now," I said. It sounded stupid, like I thought I was her mama, but I didn't know what else to say, and I wouldn't cry in front of my uncle, wouldn't let him see he'd hurt me the way he'd damaged everyone else in his life.

What also pinged was the joy and excitement in my cousin's eyes as she threw her paltry belongings into the back seat of the car. She jumped up front with her daddy. I tried to be happy for her, but she wasn't sad at all to be leaving us; she was downright triumphant. Her parents were finally coming through.

Suzie leaned out the front window to kiss Mama goodbye, and there wasn't a glint of a tear, although she did remember to say "thanks."

"You're a ring-a-ding-doozie ..." I heard Mama begin, but she choked up and couldn't finish. She stepped backward into her flower bed, not noticing the black-eyed Susans she trampled underfoot.

Suzie waved bye, and blew us kisses.

You'd have thought she was driving off with some movie star to go live in Hollywood, California, instead of across the tracks to the bad side of town to live with an old drunk and his crazy wife in some nasty house with not enough beds and nothing but greasy fried eggs to eat.

I pitied her. I admired her. Oh, how I would miss her!

Mama went back into our house saying she felt a headache coming on. I knew she'd stay in bed for the rest of the day, if not longer.

I stood at the end of the driveway, watching Uncle Travis's car get smaller and smaller until it was swallowed up by a curve some distance away. Then I shook my fist and hollered, "You be good to them girls, you hear me?"

I picked up some hickory nuts from the side of the road and threw them as hard as I could after the car. But there was no one left in the road to hit.

Eighteen

I'd always loved the good kind of alone you feel when you're by yourself in a quiet house for a few hours and you know you can do whatever you want before the rest of the family comes home and spoils the hush. That's a lot less lonely kind of alone than the kind I felt after Jimmy ran off and Daddy died and Suzie went away, when most of the chairs were full of empty and the one person left at home seemed like she wanted to be in the cold ground more than she wanted to stay with me.

This was what the bad kind of alone felt like.

It was that night, after Suzie left us, that I saw Mama take the gun from the nightstand drawer and hold it in her lap like an answer to prayer. I lay beside her in bed, searching the dark ceiling for answers of my own.

Worry consumed me. Mama had the pills the doctor gave her to calm her nerves, plenty of them. What if she took them all? Then there was the pistol ….

I had to do something, and I had to do it soon. Mama was all I had left.

Mama rolled over and swatted at the alarm clock, finally hitting the right button to stop its insistent buzzing. For a golden second everything seemed right in her world. I caught my breath and waited, dreading the moment her hand would reach across the wide expanse of bed sheets to find me instead of Daddy. Before she even turned on the lamp, I heard the hitch in her breathing that meant the weight of his death had settled on her chest. When I opened my eyes, her sweet face crumpled into a picture of pain, and she began to cry again.

God, give me strength, I prayed, out of habit, even though I no longer expected it to work.

"Do you want some breakfast?" No answer.

Her silence scared me.

She reached under her pillow where she'd tucked Daddy's pajamas the night before, pulled them out, and rocked back and forth like a child with a blanket, sobbing. She wasn't quiet now. Her pain was like a fresh cut. I cooed and patted her, to no effect. I didn't know what to say or do to make things better. Would she cry all day? We were supposed to get back to our normal routine today. Would Mama and I miss school and work altogether, or be terribly late? Long minutes ticked by before, tears spent, she rolled out of bed, folded the pajamas, and put them back in the bureau drawer. I shuddered to think of them there, wet with her tears, reeking of Daddy's sweat, stained with his blood.

"I'll make us some cereal." Mama's face was a smooth mask. Once again, she spoke as if nothing had happened. She put her pink chenille bathrobe on over her nightgown and left the room.

This ritual couldn't be helping her, I thought. And it certainly wasn't helping me, sleeping with one eye open to make sure she didn't overdose or shoot herself.

It had only been a week or so since Daddy died, and I knew we'd be sad for a long time, but this wallowing in grief couldn't be healthy. If I could give Mama just one good day, a day where she didn't wake up crying and go to sleep doing the same thing, she might get better. And she had to get better.

I bounded out of bed. I had a plan.

I snatched the nerve pills from her dresser, took them to my room, and hid them in my sock drawer. I'd give her one each night, to help her sleep, but only one, so she couldn't take too many and not wake up. I stood still, listening for Mama to call me to breakfast. All I heard was her getting the milk from the refrigerator, and the sound of my own quick, shallow breathing.

I went back into her bedroom and opened the nightstand drawer. The pistol looked evil in the morning light, a box of bullets lying beside it. I picked up the pistol by the grip and carried it, barrel pointed down at the floor, to the closet in the hall where my dresses were hung because my bedroom was too small for me to have a closet in there. The box of ammunition was heavier than I'd expected. My heart drummed in my ears.

I found my old plaid lunchbox on the floor by my shoes and tucked the pistol inside, happy to hear the two silver clasps click shut. Then I hid the ammunition on the top shelf of the hall linen closet, wrapped in an old beach towel. If she somehow found the pistol in one closet, maybe she wouldn't find the bullets in the other closet next to it. I didn't know how to check to see if the pistol was already loaded.

Mama rounded the corner of the hallway as I closed both closet doors.

"Coming, Honey?" she asked.

"Yes, Ma'am." I smiled and walked past her, toward the kitchen.

Two problems solved. That left one more, for after school.

Nineteen

I jumped off the bus at our corner, taking care not to look toward the spot where Kat had been hit by the truck. She was still in Tampa, at the Shriner's Hospital, and we almost never saw any of the Barringtons at home anymore. When they weren't at school or at work, they were with Kat.

Sometimes I ached to see her myself. But I didn't have time to think about that. I was on a mission.

I made my way up our driveway to the carport, where our rusty washing machine stood in the open air beside the steps. It was time Mama got her mourning over with. Martyrdom wasn't helping her, no matter how much she might enjoy the phone calls, flowers, cards and attention her role as the grieving widow brought. Dead calm, I carefully measured a cup of lemon-scented Tide, then opened the lid and dumped the detergent into the washer. A clean citrus smell drifted skyward.

I unlocked the kitchen door and went inside, dropping my purse, white sweater, and school books on the kitchen table. I fed Doodle the Poodle, and then let him out the back door into our fenced yard to do his business.

I walked to my mother's bedroom, so nervous that I couldn't remember which drawer she always put the pajamas in. My stomach fluttered and my hands shook as I reached toward the bureau. What was I afraid of? I was doing the right thing. Mama would surely understand.

Daddy's harmonica rested on top of the bureau. I couldn't look at it without wanting to hear its plaintive song. I thought about blowing into it, but didn't know how to play a tune, so I left it where he'd last laid it down and opened the top drawer, filled with Daddy's neatly folded white undershirts and boxer shorts. The second drawer still held his socks, some white, some dark. The blue pajamas were in the third drawer. I touched the left breast pocket where Daddy had sometimes tucked his black-framed glasses, and a vivid memory of him wearing the pajamas while reading us the Christmas story from the gospel of Luke rose unbidden to my mind.

I lifted the pajama top to my nose. It smelled of fear-sweat, blood, and my mother's stale tears. The bottoms also had rust-colored blotches mixed with what could only be patches of dried snot.

They were gross. How could she sleep with those filthy things? No wonder she was morbid. Then I felt mean. Poor Daddy. He couldn't help getting sick. He couldn't help the smell of the sweat or the blood. Those things came with a cerebral hemorrhage. Mama couldn't help her tears or runny nose, either.

I felt tears well up in my own eyes, but I blinked them back down. There was nothing I could do to find Jimmy or to bring our loved ones back from the grave. And it might be mean, but I was sure that all our sorrow was somehow wrapped up inside those nasty pajamas.

My mind was made up. There was nothing to do but get on with it.

I was almost running by the time I sailed down the kitchen steps to the carport and threw the pajamas into the washer. I banged down the lid and spun the dial to NORMAL, then yanked it out. Cold water poured into the washing machine. I climbed the stairs back into the house.

One normal day. That's all I craved. *Please, God,* for Mama and for me. A day when we didn't wake up with a huge hole where our hearts were supposed to be, where Mama didn't take a nerve pill to fall asleep, clutching the smelly pajamas Daddy died in.

From inside the kitchen, I could hear the swish-slosh of the washer that told me the pajamas were on their way to coming clean.

I smiled with satisfaction as I walked into the den.

There. Everything would be back to normal soon.

As the washing machine on the carport did its work, I rocked and rocked in the chair Daddy used to love.

I stopped rocking. The absence of sloshing and spinning told me the washer had finished its work.

Please, let them look normal.

I walked outside and opened the lid. The pajamas lay damp and crumpled on the floor of the machine. We had no dryer; the sun and fresh air did that work. I carried them to the clothesline strung along one side of our backyard. Doodle ran at my heels, jumping to see what I'd brought him. I shook the top and bottoms to smooth them, and hung them on the line with four wooden pins from the cloth bag hanging there. A startled lizard leapt from the bag to the line and raced like a tightrope walker to safety at the other end. The pajamas flapped in the light breeze like baby blue flags. The fresh hint of lemons infused the air. A couple of light bloodstains remained, but they could easily have passed for spilled coffee.

The spooky effect was gone. Mama's heart would have to be lightened, too.

At eight o'clock that night, Mama put down her book and went to take a shower. Once again curled in Daddy's chair, I was unable to focus on "The Tell-Tale Heart," the story by Edgar Allen Poe that we were assigned to read for English class. But I was so excited about the surprise I'd planned for Mama, I could certainly relate to the pounding heart.

When the bathroom door banged open, I thought my heart might stop.

Mama walked into the den, and crossed to the rocking chair to kiss me goodnight. She wore a gingham nightgown, her skin still damp and steamy from the shower. Her hair was wrapped in a towel, ready to be pin curled, and her face was scrubbed clean, with no trace of make-up. She smelled of light dusting powder and Pond's cold-cream. Good mother-smells. She was going to be so happy when she found the pajamas, with all the sadness washed out of them. Wasn't she?

"Don't stay up too late," she said. "Remember to turn all the lights off before you come to bed." Then she walked down the hall to her lonesome bedroom.

I heard the bureau drawer slide open, heard the whisper of cotton as she took the pajamas out. There was a moment of silence, during which I heard my heart as clearly as the murderer in Poe's story did.

She howled then—screamed in primordial pain. I raced down the hall like I'd been shot from the hidden pistol, to find her on her knees by the bed, keening. I stood in her doorway, silent, frozen.

She looked up at me with blazing eyes. "What did you DO?" she hissed. Her towel turban leaned to one side.

"Just … washed off … the blood …."

The light went out of her eyes as she stared at and through me. Daddy's pajamas slipped from her fingers and pooled around her where she knelt at the foot of the bed.

I moved toward her. "Mama, they were gross."

She looked away from me then, and held her arm out stiffly, stopping me.

"How could you?" Her voice was as cold as a grave. "They don't smell like him anymore."

"Please…." My voice cracked. If she would just *listen* ….

She still didn't look at me, just stared at the clean pajamas on the floor as if they were a nest of coiled rattlesnakes. "Get away from me."

I had seen her angry before, but this was worse. I had cut her too deeply. She looked deflated, like a balloon after the air had escaped. And there was nothing I could do to fix things.

The woman on the floor seemed broken, unable to even look at the one who had broken her, much less look at her with a mother's forgiving love.

How could she?

She didn't say she would never forgive me. She didn't have to.

I closed her bedroom door behind me. The soft click of the latch sounded to me like a skeleton key turning in a dungeon door, a dungeon into which no light could penetrate. Was I the warden, locking my mother inside, or was I the one being locked out, with no way to find the key?

I wandered the house, keeping busy, stacking papers and books, hanging up towels and clothes, turning off lights. I pretended that the sun would still rise in the morning, that we would both go off to work and school, that life would somehow continue.

I couldn't keep up the ruse in the face of my guilt. I felt it like a delicate thread snapping. I had destroyed the one thing she had that made it possible for her to go on living.

A terrible crash behind the wall separating my room from Mama's made me leap to my feet and fling open her door. Perfume, tissues, lotion, bobby pins, comb, brush, and mirror, all littered the carpet. She'd swept the entire contents of her dresser top to the floor. She leaned against the dresser. The wet towel fell across her shoulders; her damp hair stuck out in strange clumps. "Where are my God-damned pills?"

I had never heard her curse before in my life.

"I'll get you one," I said. I was sure she'd follow me to my room and snatch the bottle from my hand, but she didn't. When I returned with one nerve pill from my sock drawer and a glass of water from the kitchen, she sat like a docile kitten on the edge of her bed. I gave her the pill. She swallowed it. I gave her the glass of water. She sipped it, and then placed the glass on the bedside table.

"I don't know you," Mama said.

I picked up the litter from the floor and arranged her dresser the way she always kept it. She didn't stop me or send me away. Her dusting powder had spilled, so I scooped as much of it as I could from the carpet back into the box and put the lid on top. I sneezed twice, then used a tissue and tossed it into the wastebasket before putting the tissue box back on the left-hand corner of the dresser. None of the perfumes or lotions had broken, but some of the bobby pins had fallen into the powder and the room reeked of it. From the corner of my eye I saw she had kicked the pajamas under the bed. I left them there.

"I'll give you another pill in the morning, if you need it," I promised. Then I closed her door again and went to wash the powder from my hands.

Back in my bedroom, my textbooks seemed written in Swahili. The marks on the pages made no sense. I turned the pages anyway.

Doubt not, said Saint Joan in my head.

"Shut up," I said aloud.

I heard the nightstand drawer open and close behind the wall. Mama didn't ask where the pistol was. That was one thing I'd done right.

I read. I slept.

Morning came.

Part Five

1977

Twenty

It's hard to put my finger on exactly what was wrong with the way Mama treated me in the two years after I washed Daddy's pajamas. It was like living with the Tin Man from the *Wizard of Oz*, before he got a heart.

She didn't kick me out of her life, take me to the Baptist Home for Children, or deprive me of food, shelter, or education. She still sewed my clothes and bought me presents at Christmas, Easter and my birthday. When I turned sixteen, she gave me a used, navy blue Ford Pinto. She even started giving me a quick peck on the cheek and wishing me goodnight again, after a while. It was like being kissed by a ghost.

Since that awful night, we each slept in our own rooms. I hadn't realized how much I enjoyed stretching out alone in bed until I was able to do it again.

She stopped slapping me like when I was a little kid, and we took care of the house and the chores together, like always, except that she turned laundry duty over to me completely, as if the washing machine itself had conspired with me and was somehow her enemy.

"You're so good at washing clothes—it's your job now," she said.

Some days we were barely civil to each other. Other days it seemed almost like old times. She even made jokes now and then.

But she always stopped short when she found herself laughing or having any kind of fun—as if mourning was her job now, and she was determined to be good at it.

There was a wall between us that maybe only I could see. Mama seemed to fold in on herself like an origami bird, as different from my real mother as the Oriental paper version was to a real crane.

Dr. Holland gave her nerve pills that got her through the day, and arranged for her to consult a psychologist who specialized in helping widows "navigate the grieving process." I was full of hope and excitement when Mama went to her first appointment with Dr. Chiozza, but she came into the house that evening, tossed her purse on the couch, and announced, "That man's crazier than I am." She never went back.

Her headaches crippled her, and there were long days that passed, end upon end, where she emerged from her dark bedroom only to stumble to the toilet and back again, calling weakly for BC Powders mixed in tepid tea, with occasional bites of buttered toast.

True to form, I tried my best to make things right by being better than good, as if I could earn my way back into Mama's good graces. It didn't work, of course, and frustrated that I couldn't make her well and happy, I felt like a failure.

One day a letter arrived from Shriner's Hospital in Tampa. I tore into it like a starving child would rip open a candy bar. The words were written in spidery cursive pencil.

Hey, Bee.

Mama is writing this letter for me while I tell her what to say.

Thank you for sending me the crayons and the coloring books with all the pictures of flowers in them. Don't worry, I don't think they are babyish, even though they are the fat kind we used in first grade. My hands are working better than my legs, but like Lucy told you, I can't hold the skinny crayons good yet.

Mrs. Hopkins comes every day to help me with my school work. She says reading is hard for me because the letters get all jumbled between the page and my eyes and my brain. She's helping me to read and write better. We are reading Little Women, *because I know it's your favorite.*

Everyone is real nice here, except it really hurts when they make me work on learning to walk again in PT. But I try very hard.

I pray for all of you every day, and hope you pray for me. Your Daddy is still my hero, and you will always be my best friend.

The letter was signed *K-A-T* in purple crayon.

Mama wanted me to study my Bible, like I used to, but instead I checked out stacks and stacks of poetry books from the library and read them from cover to cover. Some of them rhymed and some of them didn't, and some of them I didn't even understand. I just liked the way the words sounded in my head.

I made excuses for not going to church. Mama wasn't happy about it, but she'd let me stay home if I claimed I was overloaded with homework or had a special school project coming due.

One Wednesday evening, while Mama was dressing for prayer meeting, Brother Dimmesdale stopped by our house on his way to church. I invited him into the kitchen and said I'd go get Mama, but he put his hand on my arm and said, "No, I'm here to visit with you." His voice was as pretty as ever, and it felt nice where his skin touched mine, but when he saw me staring at his hand, he quickly let go. I flushed red.

"We've missed you at church, Honey," he began. He looked like a blend of Butch Cassidy *and* the Sundance Kid—a Robert Redford face with Paul Newman's eyes.

Perfection. I watched his mouth as he talked, leaning easily against the table. "I know it's been hard on you without your Daddy and your brother, but you've been real helpful to your Mama, real brave."

I was barefoot, wearing shorts and a tied up boy-shirt. He stared into my eyes for as long as he could, but then his glance slipped down, toward the rest of me. He stared at the motorcycle scar on my leg.

By now I knew his wife wouldn't conveniently die and that even if she did, he was too old for me. I no longer wanted to marry him—I just wanted to kiss him.

"Jimmy used to tell me to face my fear, and the death of fear would come," I murmured.

"Jimmy was right. With the Lord by our side, we can face our fears and overcome anything," he said.

"I think you're right," I said, taking a step closer. "I don't think there's anything I'm afraid of."

Longing as ancient as Jezebel's must have shone on my face because he took a half step back, but the wall was in his way. He looked like he was afraid the Lord might be on vacation.

"Well, hope to see you next Sunday," he said, and slipped sideways out the door.

He hustled down the driveway, almost running, like a man who was scared to death. I snorted. "Fear not, Brother Warren."

While Mama was at prayer meeting I washed the supper dishes. Putting away the deviled eggs dish in the china hutch, I came across the old ashtray with the plastic donkey on it that Paw Paw had used when he visited us. My fashion conscious mother, so meticulous with her housekeeping and conservative in her home décor, found the little burro embarrassing and always hid him there when Paw Paw wasn't around. I was surprised she hadn't pitched it by now, but decided sentiment must have won out over good taste.

I set it up on the kitchen table and lifted the tail. No cigarette emerged, which didn't surprise me. Mama would have thrown those out, first thing, after Paw Paw died. I pulled back the ears, and a match popped out. I lit it and watched it burn, and then dropped it into the ashtray. I lit another. The flame was beautiful, but too small, gone too fast.

I grabbed a napkin from the holder and lit that, dropping it into the glass ashtray. Much better. But it, too, was gone too quickly. And how would I explain the odor of smoke in the house?

I grabbed air freshener from under the sink and sprayed it in a flowery cloud, then looked around the house for something else to burn.

In Mama's desk I found a stack of old Bible drill ribbons. I snatched up four or five (she'd never notice those missing) and took them and the ashtray outside to the back steps. The ribbons didn't flame nicely, though, just sort of melted and singed brown around the edges.

There was quite a little pile in the bowl of the ashtray now, but my excitement was only growing.

What else? I went back inside the house and walked from room to room.

From the sconce on the wall in the hall, I grabbed a chunky white candle. From a basket of seashells on the table in the den, a handful of straw. And from the Bible in my room, I plucked a little card that had nestled between the pages for years.

I sat on step six, halfway up and halfway down, overlooking Bass River, which was about to swallow the sun, and set the candle in the ashtray on top of the half-burned Bible drill ribbons. I swirled the straw around the candle, higher and higher, until only the wick protruded at the top.

The donkey spit the match into my hand. I raked it across his back and then lit the candle. The flame burned small and bright. I dropped the match onto the straw, and gasped at the *whoosh* as the dry tinder caught. The donkey's plastic tail began to melt. I didn't care.

I lifted the card above the pyre and admired it one last time by the glow of the flames. Saint Joan of Arc on her stallion lifted her battle flag as proudly as ever. It didn't matter how brave you were, I thought. Always, after the miracles, came the cross, or the stake. I lowered her into the ashtray and watched, mesmerized, as she burned.

Twenty-One

My high school home economics teacher, Mrs. Allen, didn't think much of me, and the feeling was mutual. She was nice enough, but she didn't seem to understand that a girl like me, who was going to be a famous journalist someday, didn't need to learn what she called "the domestic arts." It was 1977, after all, and plenty of women had careers. But at Ed White High School, Home Economics was still mandatory for one semester, and I'd already waited until the last half of my junior year to take it. The rest of the class consisted of silly freshman girls who got all fluttery over biscuits, cookies, and casseroles that featured cream-of-something soup and dried onions. I considered kitchen work a necessary evil.

But cookies and casseroles were a cake walk compared to our sewing project. Mama, a talented seamstress who'd delighted in making clothes for our family and curtains for our home, always said that when the angels were handing out sewing talent, I thought they'd said "snowing" and stayed inside, where it was warm. Funny, since it had never snowed in Jacksonville that I could remember.

Mrs. Allen had assigned our sewing project a week before, and Mama seemed to get a small kick out of taking me to The Old Sew and Sew to buy a Butterick bibbed apron pattern and a yard of lavender cotton. It was the first fun thing we'd done together in a long time, and I felt cautiously optimistic. We'd gotten as far as cutting out the pattern and pinning it to the fabric when Mama got sick again with one of her migraines. I hadn't touched the apron all week, because I was sure I'd mess it up without her supervision.

I didn't think about the apron again until the project deadline snuck up on me. Unlike the old days, I'd grown very scatterbrained about my schoolwork, especially due dates.

Several of the girls walked into Home Ec that day with finished aprons. Mrs. Allen's face, the color of cool chocolate milk, beamed with happiness. She loved that domestic stuff.

"Remember, class, the assignment was to create a memory apron decorated to represent stories from your life. The purpose was to learn to cut to a pattern, and sew a fine hand stitch."

Mrs. Allen asked for a volunteer to exhibit her apron to the class. Hands waved in the air. She called on Debbie Avery, who held up a yellow apron with stars in different colors and patterns circling the hem. "These stars are cut from each of my little brothers' baby blankets," she said. "I have five brothers, so far. We call them the Avery All-Stars. Daddy says he's not stopping till he has his own baseball team."

I didn't ask out loud, but I wondered what her mother thought about that. Didn't you have to have nine kids for a baseball team? Nine! Or was that just the number of innings in a game?

The next girl, Allison Leroux, had flags from several countries sewn on her red, white, and blue striped apron. My sense of order was offended by the haphazard placement of the flag patches. I'd have spaced them out nice and even, in a straight line around the bottom. She must have been scared of snow on talent day, too, from the look of her jagged stitches. But she slipped that apron on and sashayed in front of the class like a fashion model. "These flags are from the countries we've visited on vacation. We save up all year and go to a new place each time. But my best memories are from right here in the USA, so that's why my apron looks like our flag."

Well, ain't she a Yankee Doodle Dandy? I was as patriotic as the next kid, but her perky patter got on my nerves. Not everybody got to travel around the world. Not everybody had a mom and a dad to take her on vacation.

Some of us were lucky if our mamas got out of bed in the morning and didn't shoot themselves. I rolled my eyes and sighed.

Uh-oh. Mrs. Allen saw me. She left her perch on the edge of her desk and walked toward me.

"Honey, is your apron ready today?" she asked in her *I don't like your attitude* voice. Was she blind? Did she see an apron on my table?

She might not be my favorite teacher, but I didn't want to lie to her outright.

"It's not quite ready yet," I said. "I'm having a little trouble deciding which memories to choose." That was an understatement, since my most vivid, notable lifetime memory was of Daddy's funeral. Maybe I could choose a cheery tombstone motif.

"Well, the project's due tomorrow, so I suggest you get busy," Mrs. Allen said.

She walked back to her desk, turned, and smiled at me.

"Start by thinking about the most fun day you've ever had," she suggested.

My most fun day will be the day I finish this class, I thought. But after school, I forced myself to do what she suggested, because I couldn't let myself fail Mrs. Allen's class if I wanted to get a scholarship to journalism school. How ironic if a future prize-winning reporter got derailed by a stupid sewing project. First I'd get an F on the memory apron. Then I'd flunk Home Ec and never graduate high school. Soon I'd be living in a cardboard box and eating cat food. That would prove Mama right, when she said I should learn how to sew, wouldn't it? But how was I going to finish the apron by the next day?

I threw my books and purse onto the front seat of the Pinto and said a prayer to whoever the patron saint of clunkers might be as I pumped the gas and turned the key. It started.

As I inched my way out of the school parking lot, I tried to figure out the most fun I'd ever had. I closed my eyes for a moment in the slow-moving line of student traffic and thought of the word "fun." The picture that popped into my mind was the weekend I was ten, when we sewed holes together to make a cast net, then fished as a family foursome on the beach.

By the time the Pinto wheezed to a stop in the parking lot of Harper's Bait and Tackle, I'd decided I'd cut some gray fabric into the shape of a fish to decorate my memory apron. I would use one of the scraps from Mama's sewing basket. It was a start.

Twenty-Two

Most days since I'd been old enough to drive a car instead of riding the bus, I stopped by the store on the way home from school to see Maw Maw. Usually I just needed a little bucking up.

That day there were three pickup trucks, two with boat trailers hitched to the back, parked in the sand parking lot alongside the white Cadillac Maw Maw had bought with some of Paw Paw's life insurance money. "Your Paw Paw always wanted me to have nice things," I recalled her explaining when the family first saw her drive up in the brand-new Caddy, even though none of us could recollect him buying her any while he was living.

The car wasn't the only thing that had changed about Maw Maw. As I plopped down on the barstool at the counter near the cash register, I saw that the metal ashtray was full of Virginia Slims butts, as usual, but now they were decorated on one end with little half-moons of pink lipstick. Her silver-gray hair was brushed out in soft curls over her shoulders instead of cinched into her usual tight ponytail. And, Lord have mercy, was she actually wearing a *dress*? Just a plaid cotton house-shift, but still.

"Close your mouth before something flies in there, Stink-bait," she said, reminding me, with a pang, of my daddy.

I grinned and tried to wolf whistle. "I see you've got some nice bait, Miz Harper, but I can't tell what you're fishing for." The handful of fishermen who belonged to the rigs outside chuckled. They smelled like a mixture of river mud, sweat, and beer. Maw Maw either didn't notice or didn't mind.

"You ain't too big for me to bend over my knee, young lady. Besides, Katherine Hepburn said it best: If you want to trade the admiration of many men for the criticism of one, just get married."

"Didja hear that, Duke?" yelled one of the men, slapping the bar. The quietest, best-looking one of the bunch took the last swallow of his bottle of beer, nodded his ball cap at Maw Maw, mumbled, "Ma'am, Miss," in our direction, and left the store. I was pretty sure I saw him wink at Maw Maw on his way out. The others paid for their purchases and filed out behind him, leaving me and Maw Maw alone.

Maw Maw watched the one named Duke all the way out the door, across the porch, and into his truck, and her eyes shone like I imagined mine did when I passed one particularly tall, sandy-haired surfer dude launching his racing shell in Bass River on my way to school each morning. Old people. They were so cute.

"It's like bees to honeysuckle, once a man smells an independent woman he thinks might have a little spending cash. Still, they do help pass the time of day."

She rinsed the empty bottles and put them in the return case with a clink, then swished a wet rag along the bar before pulling her stool up across from where I sat. We could talk there, and she wouldn't have to get up to ring up the next customer who came in.

"How's your Mama, Honey?"

"Same as usual." I sighed. "Most days she's got a headache, but even when she isn't hurting, she just doesn't want to DO anything, you know? She's got no pep."

"Well, how are you holding up, then? How's school?" Maw Maw hopped down from her perch, popped the top off a bottle of Yoo-hoo, and plopped it and a circus wagon shaped box of animal crackers in front of me before I could even mention I was starving. I noticed her legs were smooth and tanned, with visible muscles, and I tried to remember if I'd ever seen her bare legs before, but all I could conjure up were memories of her in dungarees.

I liked coming here after school, answering the questions that Mama no longer cared to ask. This strong, capable woman, also a widow, seemed so alive by contrast, and so interested in me and my life.

"I've gotta finish my memory apron tonight. It's due tomorrow, and I have a feeling Mrs. Allen is gonna call on me first."

"What in tarnation is a memory apron?" Maw Maw's brow furrowed.

I explained the concept, and her eyes softened. "You got any ideas?"

I looked around the store and shrugged. "Well, I'll have to have a fish patch, now won't I?"

"I reckon so." She nibbled on an elephant cracker while I bit the head off a lion. "What else?"

"I don't know, Maw Maw. I mean, how do you decide, out of a whole lifetime, what's important to remember, and what's not? I know this for sure—there are things I don't want to remember, things I'd just as soon forget ever happened."

Maw Maw lit a cigarette, inhaled and blew a perfect smoke ring. I didn't like the smell, but the effect was oddly fetching. "Like losing your daddy and Paw Paw?" she murmured. "Or Jimmy and Kat and Suzie all moving away?"

I shook my head. "No, in fact, I think I'll add a playhouse patch for Kat. In her last letter, she said she's doing real well, and might be home in time for graduation." I scrunched my forehead, thinking hard. "It's more like … regrets. Things I've done that I wish I could undo." I took a swig of my Yoo-hoo. "Do you have any regrets like that, Maw Maw?"

Maw Maw stared over my shoulder, past the shelves of sundries, out the window, and I could tell she was looking far beyond the parking lot to the distant past. Her eyes looked naked, raw, and for a moment I saw a flash of pain fill them. Then a shadow covered the pain, and she spoke.

"Everybody has things they'd do over if they could, Stink-bait." She smoked a little more, and then stubbed the cigarette out as if the taste of it had gone bad. She pulled a half bottle of beer from the other side of the cash register, and I realized she must have been drinking with her customers and stashed it there when I came in the store. It made me feel grown up that she was drinking beer in front of me—like she trusted me. My intuition told me she was about to reveal something she hadn't told anyone else for a long time. Maybe never.

I fingered a couple of animal crackers, but didn't eat them. Maw Maw's voice was a low hum.

"You were fifteen when your daddy died, and that's a year older than your mama was when her mother stepped into the path of that car."

My breath caught. Was I finally going to hear the truth about the death of my real grandmother?

"It nearly killed me, seeing you after your Daddy's funeral, all big pain-filled eyes and questions with no answers. You looked just the way she did, back when I married your Paw Paw." She knocked back a long slug of beer. "She blamed me, you know."

I gave a quick nod, not of agreement, but of encouragement. Go on.

"I was young, I was divorced, I had two daughters who were getting too big for their britches, and I fell in love with a man who was married to someone else." She raised her eyes to meet mine and stared at me with defiance. "It was wrong, but it didn't feel that way. I don't expect you to understand that, and I hope you never have to be the 'other woman,' but it's true." She patted the back of my hand, where I spun a cookie giraffe on the countertop. "People find a way to justify doing what they want to do, Honey. Everybody is the hero of their own movie."

I secretly hoped that I'd love someone so much someday that I wouldn't care what the rules were, either. But I didn't mention that to Maw Maw.

Instead, I asked the question that had been burning inside me for years. "Do you think Grandma's death was an accident, Maw Maw?"

"Thomas said she'd figured out why I was always hanging out at the store, why he was always disappearing for hours at a time, and she was yelling at him and crying and just stepped off that curb … never saw what hit her. He always said that's what happened, and I never doubted his story."

I took Maw Maw's hand in mine on top of the bar. "Do you think Mama believed Paw Paw, or do you think she thinks he pushed her?"

Maw Maw's eyes grew wide. "Did she tell you that?"

"No, Ma'am. But she don't seem to trust nobody, especially men. I just wondered if that's where it came from. I mean, if you think your Daddy killed your Mama …."

"I'm sure that for a long time she thought Paw Paw and I had hatched a plan to kill your grandma and run off together. I'll never forget her silence, and those big blue eyes watching, always watching me." Maw Maw shuddered, and sipped the last swallow of beer. She picked at the bottle's label with one unpainted fingernail. "Later on, she learned to love me. That's the way she is. She loves, but she doesn't trust. She wants to keep her world small and safe. That's why she's so bossy. But that's a tough way to live, because people don't like to be controlled. You can never really control anyone but yourself, and that's hard enough."

I pushed an animal cracker across the bar to Maw Maw and she picked it up and ate it. I chewed on one myself, without tasting it. My mama didn't even have the strength to control herself anymore, much less try to run anyone else's life.

The door of the store opened and a man and his wife walked in, bickering and asking directions. Maw Maw smiled and consulted their crumpled map and sent them on their way with a MoonPie and a Nutty Buddy.

"Do you think Paw Paw could have done it?" I asked, as soon as they were out the door. She gave me a sharp look, and I added, "I mean, you weren't there, so how could you know for sure?"

Maw Maw sighed, and her shoulders drooped as she settled back onto her bar stool. I could see she'd chewed her lipstick off since we'd started talking. "After we got married and he and your mama and Travis moved in with me and my girls, I found out what a mean bastard your Paw Paw could be."

I'd never seen him act vicious, but her story had the ring of truth and confirmed what my mama'd always said about her daddy.

"I'd heard rumors that he used to get drunk and beat his wife and kids, but he was so different with me—funny, charming. I didn't see what I didn't want to believe."

Maw Maw paused her story long enough to wrap up a pound of shrimp on ice for Herb, the man who mowed her lawn, and send him on his way.

"One night not long after we got married, he stayed out late, came home drunk, and slapped me across the mouth when I spoke up about it."

I thought about Mama's penchant for face-slapping, the shame and humiliation of it that stung worse than the blow did.

"I did as I was told. I quietly went to bed, and then when he was passed out good and cold beside me, I crept to the kitchen and got the butcher knife."

My eyes grew wide as I imagined the scene. How scared and desperate she must have been!

She chuckled. "Paw Paw woke up with that knife pressed against his jugular vein. I told him, real cool-like, if he ever raised his hand to me or one of the kids in my house again, he'd wake up in the funeral parlor." She smirked. "I told him he was a mean bastard, and he'd been raised by a long line of mean bastards, and I knew he was trying to prove he was the meanest bastard of them all. But I'd fallen in love with his good side, and I'd respect him more if he'd be man enough to show his good side to the rest of the world."

"Bless your heart," I said, shaking my head, meaning she was one crazy lady and that was one risky move.

"He still drank after that, but he never hit another living soul until the day he died."

She stared out the window again, and then barked a strange, hollow laugh. "I reckon if he'd had it in him to kill a wife, he would have killed me that night."

I walked around the bar and put my arms around her, laid my head on her shoulder. "I'm glad he didn't take that knife away and use it on you, Maw Maw."

She kissed me on the top of my head. "People will push you around, if you let them, Stink-bait. And life will knock you down. But if you get up again, if you don't quit, you haven't failed."

I looked up at her. "Do you think Mama's quit on me, Maw Maw?"

She shook her head. "Your Mama wants to quit sometimes, but she's got too much of Paw Paw's fight in her. That gal's a survivor, just like you. I ain't never seen her quit on somebody she loves, and she loves you something fierce."

I wanted so badly to believe those words, but couldn't help remembering the night I saw the light of love drain out of my mama's eyes after I washed Daddy's pajamas. I couldn't tell Maw Maw about that. It still hurt too much and I was too ashamed.

Maw Maw took my hands in hers. "Your mama has lost her way. She'd have a hissy fit if she heard me call her lost, her being such a church goer and all, and she'd tell you right quick that I'm the one who's lost, with my cigarettes and beer."

She shook another Virginia Slims from the pack and lit up. "It comforts your Mama to think God is watching over her and that all her pain has been part of a plan that she just can't understand yet." She blew smoke down and away from me. "On the other hand, I think our lives are what they are because of the choices we make. Some of those choices we'd go back and change, if we could, like you mentioned earlier. But we can't. So we do the best we can with what we believe at the time."

"But what if we mess up, really badly?" I asked.

"Everybody messes up, gal. Me, you, even your mama. You learn from your mistakes, if you're smart, and you don't repeat them. But you don't let the regret of old mistakes make you too afraid to go make new ones."

I gave Maw Maw another hug and moved to get my belongings from the bar. "I think your next mistake might go by the name of Duke, don't you?" I teased her.

I skittered out the door before she could throw her shoe at me.

The last place I wanted to go was home, to face the endless well of neediness that was my cold, depressed mother. But the Pinto drove me there, as if it had a mind of its own.

Twenty-Three

When I got home, I was happily surprised to find that Mama must have been feeling better and had, in fact, made up her bed before leaving me a note on the kitchen table that read: *I have wonderful news. We'll celebrate tonight. Went in for a half-day's shift.*

I wondered what "wonderful news," had gotten her up out of bed and in the mood to work. Mama's boss at JC Penney's had a little crush on her, and therefore put up with her frequent absences due to migraine headaches, but thank goodness we had Daddy's life insurance to live on, because when Mama didn't work, she didn't get paid. I was still cleaning the judo club and had started doing some typing for Mr. Davis, the owner, after school, but he didn't pay much.

After I let Doodle outside, I settled in at the dining room table to get my homework done. The load was light, and I finished in an hour, thank Heaven, since the big challenge of the evening would be the memory apron. It was do-or-die time.

I thought about the memory aprons the other girls had brought to class.

Had my family ever been that normal, safe, and happy? Vivid, happy memories came back to me, of the art museum, church suppers, the beach.

Could I make complicated patches for the memory apron? Probably not. Too hard, since I lacked the skill with the scissors. But the memories made me smile, just the same.

I was cutting out simple patches from scraps of fabric I'd found at the bottom of Mama's sewing basket when she walked in the kitchen door with a bag full of supper from the Krystal. Mama had never liked to cook, although she had done plenty of it, and now that it was just the two of us, she simply didn't do it much. I walked into the kitchen and took the bag from her hand so she could close the door.

"Set the table and fix us an RC while I change clothes," she said. Even with fast food takeout, Mama liked a full place setting complete with silverware and napkins.

She walked the long way around, through the den, to her bedroom. On her way, I heard her stop and let Doodle in the house. He'd been huddled on the top step, whining and scratching at the back door. I'd been too preoccupied to notice.

The aroma of mustard, pickles and onions wafted from the bag as I jumped to comply with Mama's order. The white buns were soft and warm when I pulled the cheeseburgers from their little boxes, and I added extra salt to the French fries I poured onto my plate. My mouth watered, and Doodle sat up on his haunches and whined. I laughed, pinched off a corner of burger, and tossed it to him. He snuffled on the floor for it, gulped it down, and yipped his thanks. Then he resumed his begging stance.

"Nope—that's all you get. These burgers are tiny enough without you eating half of mine."

Mama liked her fries smothered in catsup, so I got the bottle of Heinz from the fridge. I cracked a tray of ice into the sink, filled two glasses, and poured us both some Royal Crown Cola.

Mama came in, tying her bathrobe over her gingham nightgown, which was what she almost always wore around the house now. She still smelled faintly of the Chanel No. Five she'd dabbed on her wrists before work.

She dove in for a sudden kiss on my cheek, and said in a playful tone, "Did you hear what our new peanut-picking President went and did the day after his inauguration?"

I knew she meant Jimmy Carter, a soft-spoken Southern Baptist farmer from up the road in Plains, Georgia, who had recently unseated President Nixon's successor, Gerald Ford. "No, ma'am, what?"

Her eyes sparkled. "He's issued a *full and unconditional pardon* to over ten thousand young men who evaded the Vietnam War draft!"

I didn't dare hope it meant what I hoped it meant. "You mean—Jimmy—"

"Can come home whenever he likes," she finished my unspoken wish. "He told me on the phone today that he'll start hitchhiking home in the morning."

"Where's he been?"

"He only had enough money for a three-minute call, so he didn't give me details. He said he'd tell us all about it when he gets home."

We squealed, held hands, and jumped up and down like first-graders. "Let's eat!" Mama roared in triumph.

She noticed I'd set the kitchen table. "Why aren't we eating in the dining room?"

"I've got my apron spread out in there. It's due tomorrow, and it looks like your sewing box exploded on the table. I raided it for scraps and then cut out memory patches, like you said I could."

"Did you come up with some good ones?"

"Yes, Ma'am. I've got all different colors."

She shook her head. "Not scraps—I meant memories. Did you come up with some good memories?"

I nodded. "I did it a little differently, though. Instead of specific events, I cut out patches that reminded me of the people I want to remember."

Mama smiled. "Good idea. It's the people that count."

"Do you remember the day we first cast for mullet, at the beach, and you cooked them with the Vidalias in the fire pit?"

Her eyes misted over. "Yes."

"I thought I'd make a gray fish for Daddy and a white onion for you," I said.

Mama smiled. "That was a good day."

I nodded, dipping a couple of my salty fries in the catsup on her plate.

"Maybe I could help you come up with some more ideas, if you get stuck."

I smiled, pleased with her offer, and nodded. "Maybe you could help with the sewing, too."

She shook her head, stood up, and rinsed her plate in the sink. "That would be cheating. Mrs. Allen is not interested in how well your mother can sew."

"I was afraid you'd say that." I washed both our dishes and stacked them in the dish drainer to air-dry. We moved to the dining room and I picked up the apron pattern, still pinned to the lavender cotton. Mama grabbed her sewing basket and opened its hinged top.

I was amazed to see Mama up and about, even smiling. It felt wonderful to have her help with my sewing project, even if all she did was sit at the table and encourage me.

"Here goes nothing," I said.

Twenty-Four

Mama handed me the sharp sewing scissors from her basket and watched while I carefully cut the fabric in the shape of the pattern pieces we'd pinned there the week before. Then she showed me how to lay the apron pieces out on the table and pin them together the way they looked in the drawing on the back of the pattern envelope. There were basically four pieces: the apron skirt, the bib, and two sashes—a small one that looped around the neck and a longer, wider one to tie at the waist. There was a pocket we could sew on for extra credit, but I had a feeling the basic design would be hard enough. The picture on the front of the pattern showed the whole thing trimmed in ric-rac. I purely hated ric-rac.

"Why don't you cut the edges with the pinking shears? It looks artsy, and you won't have to hem it," Mama said.

I tried it and grinned. She was right. The zig-zagged edges looked cool.

All pinned together, it looked more like a real apron.

Maybe this was doable, after all. I settled into a dining room chair across from Mama and threaded a needle with pretty lavender thread. I poked my thumb first thing, yelled "Shoot!" and stuck it into my mouth to suck the drop of blood at the tip, so Mama jumped up to give me a thimble.

"You don't want to bleed on the fabric," she said.

I laughed. "I could bleed all over it, and tell Mrs. Allen I wanted to share my memories of the war." Then I bit my lip, knowing I'd stepped on Mama's excitement about Jimmy.

Her glance was sharp. "What kind of patch did you make to remember your brother?" she asked.

I plucked a green scrap from the pile on the table. "This color made me think of the mountains he loved. I made a peace sign."

Mama nodded. "Makes sense."

"It was hard to cut out."

"I'll bet."

"It's weird, with him a black belt and all, that he didn't want to fight. I mean, I don't think he took off because he was scared, do you?"

"Your brother wasn't scared of anything. He just didn't want to kill people for a cause he didn't believe in."

I began sewing the apron skirt to the bib. My stitches were hesitant, but smoothed out a little as I made progress across the long, straight seam. I could see that Mama's hands itched to take the apron from me and do it better and faster, but she kept them busy straightening the mess on the table instead.

"You know who always liked a good fight?" I said, smiling. "Kat. I made a red playhouse patch for her. Remember the day I kicked her butt for being a bully?"

Mama stopped sorting the spools of thread I'd dumped from the sewing basket onto the table top in my haste to find the scraps for my patches.

"Don't speak ill of your friend, Honey."

"I'm not criticizing her, Mama, I'm just telling the truth."

"Well, bless her heart, she's not here to defend herself, now is she?"

I stabbed the needle in and out of the fabric, in a crude imitation of Mama's easy style. "I don't get why you do that all the time."

"Do what?" Her voice was brittle.

"I dunno, exactly." I thought hard for a minute, and then tried again. "It seems like, once somebody dies or moves away, you forget all about what they were really like. You make them into some kind of saint or something."

Mama scowled and threw a few random spools into the basket. "I don't know what you're talking about."

The skirt and bib were together now, so I pulled the pins out and stuck them in Mama's pin cushion, shaped like a fat red tomato. I started sewing the short neck loop, really just a roll of fabric we'd pinned to two sides of the bib.

"Like Kat, for instance. She used to beat me up all the time, but after the accident, you talked about her like she was the sweetest child who ever lived."

Mama snorted. "I don't find it respectful or necessary to bring up a person's bad side, once they've been paid back by fate. At that point, it's a little late for them to change the past, you know? And she was just a child. Some folks grow out of their meanness, given time."

"But you did the same thing with Paw Paw, and he was old. You used to warn us not to ride in the car with him, because he drank so bad. But now that he's dead, all you talk about when someone mentions him is the big donation he made to our church in his will."

"Lots of people change their ways at the end, when they feel death approaching, Honey. And that donation was a good thing for him to do, to try to make up a little for … for some things he did that weren't so nice." Mama tapped her fingers on the table top in a nervous staccato rhythm.

I poked the needle into the long sash, where it was pinned over the seam that held the bib to the skirt. As I talked, I kept sewing. "You did the same thing with Daddy."

Her eyes narrowed, she stopped tapping, and spoke in an almost-whisper. "What are you talking about? He didn't have a mean bone in his body."

"Never mind." I wished I'd never brought it up.

"Oh, don't stop now," she said in a chilly voice.

Doodle whined under the table.

Outside the window, a motorcycle roared down Bass River Road, moving fast, reminding me of the day Mama pierced my ears. The old scar on my shin ached and I wished I was on that bike. Its noise faded as I spoke up again.

"I just mean that you talk to people about Daddy as if y'all never had a care in the world. But I can remember y'all fighting—a lot."

Mama stared at me as if I'd grown an extra eye in the middle of my forehead.

"We had our little disagreements, as married people do from time to time."

My needle flew. I tucked my head and watched the uneven stitches follow, one after the other. The apron was almost done.

"You talked about divorcing him."

Mama gasped and jumped up. "That's a lie! I loved him more than anything, and I would never have divorced him." She rapped the table top.

I stopped sewing. The last sloppy inches would have to be pulled and redone. Scissors in hand, I tugged out my ragged stitches. She really did rewrite history when she wanted to. She believed her own lie.

"I know how much you loved him, Mama. Sometimes I think you loved him so much, you had no more room in your heart to love anybody else."

Mama's eyes grew broad, shining with unshed tears. "Are you accusing me of not loving my children?" she whispered.

I felt hot tears fill my own eyes.

"It's obvious you love Jimmy," I said.

Mama flinched as if I had slapped her face. I couldn't stop myself. The jealous rage of all my years bubbled over.

"The one thing that's made you happy and got you out of your sick-bed, was news that your precious *son* is coming home!"

Part of me felt like a monster. But part of me thrilled to finally be the one inflicting pain. Drunk with power, I said more.

"And I think when Daddy died, you loved him so much, you wanted to die and be with him, rather than live and be with me. I've never been enough to fill that hole he left inside you. But you know what? He didn't fill you up, either. That's why y'all fought all the time."

Mama's mouth opened, but no words came out. I held out my hands. The scissor waved, imploring.

"Why is it that you're so easy on everybody else, but you never, ever cut me any slack? Yet, all this time, who's the one who stuck by you? Who's the one who cooked and cleaned for you and gave you your pills for your headaches and pills for your nerves? Do I have to die or run off before you'll decide I'm worth loving?"

Fury blinded me. I jabbed the scissors into the apron pooled on the table top.

"You loved Daddy's old pajamas more than me!"

Mama snatched the sewing scissors from the torn apron and dashed from the room. Oh, God. What was she going to do with them?

I had no strength to follow her, no will left to prevent whatever would happen next. No prayers left my lips, not to God, not to Jesus, not to Saint Joan. I was weary to the bone of playing the peacemaker, of trying to save my mother from herself.

Her bedroom door opened and then slammed, an angry sound.

I sat, frozen.

It was like Maw Maw said. You couldn't control other people, and when you tried, even for their own good, they hated you for it, because no one likes to be controlled.

Que sera, sera, like the song. *Whatever will be, will be.*

As if in a dream, Mama's borrowed sewing needle kept my trembling hands busy. First the re-stitching, small and even, then the memory patches. The brown patch was for the hickory nut I'd thrown as Uncle Travis's car drove away with Suzannah inside. A crude yellow shrimp was for Maw Maw's and Paw Paw's bait and tackle store. Red playhouse, gray fish, and white onion. One by one, memories of the people I'd loved covered the front of the apron's skirt.

I stitched on the green peace sign, repeating the magic words three times.

Jimmy. Jimmy. Jimmy. Come home. Come home. Come home.

I. Need. You.

Then it hit me. Oh, God. Had Mama even told Jimmy that Daddy was dead? Or would that impossibly hard task fall to me? I could believe she might be capable of keeping the news from him, luring him home, and making me spring it on him.

My hand moved automatically to the next patch in the stack—a cross I'd cut out from the same scrap of material as the brown hickory nut. I picked it up and hesitated. Did I still want the symbol for Christ on my apron, after he'd failed to give me a miracle for my Daddy? What, if anything, did I still believe? Maybe I should sew a big question mark instead.

I jabbed the needle into the cross, where Jesus' right armpit would have been, and quickly stitched down, around, and up, following its contours until I was back where I began. I asked myself hard questions. Did I believe in God? The answer was yes. Someone bigger than ourselves had certainly created the world and all the wonders in it. Even something as simple as flowers in a field or seashells on a beach convinced me a Master Artist had scattered them there for our delight. Did I believe Jesus was the Son of God? Yes, again, although I'd come to believe at the ripe old age of seventeen that He was one of many Children of God, which put me at odds with my fellow Baptists down at the church.

Did I believe, any longer, that I could place an order for a miracle in exchange for blind faith; that I was somehow singled out, like Saint Joan, more special than anyone else, immune to the sorrow life had to offer? Absolutely, emphatically, tragically, *no*.

I still prayed. Did I believe anyone heard me? I did not know. I hoped so.

The patch I sewed on last, the one that stood for me, was a single blue dewdrop. Or was it a tear?

The hardest thing I'd ever done was to look at Mama's closed bedroom door and not approach it. Instead, I poked a finger through the jagged holes the scissors had made in the fabric, and knew I couldn't fix Mama any more than I could make the holes my anger had torn disappear. I had to let her work things out for herself. I'd heard no sound coming through the door while I sewed and then packed the last of the scraps and spools and thimbles away in the basket. The finished apron lay, neatly folded, on the table.

I carried Mama's sewing basket back to its place in the linen closet in the hall, and then opened my clothes closet, right beside it, to get my little travel iron to press the new apron. The iron was on my closet shelf, next to my old plaid lunchbox. I stared at the box, trying to figure out what was wrong. Then it hit me. The clasps were in the open position. When I'd hidden Daddy's pistol there, so long ago, I'd latched them securely down. I snatched open the top and stared down into the empty lunchbox.

Mama opened her bedroom door behind me, and I jumped.

"Looking for something?" she asked.

She must have known, all those years, where I'd hidden Daddy's pistol, or else she'd found it later and never confronted me. My secret had become her secret in some sort of twisted dance.

"Is this what you're looking for?" she asked, turning back into her room and opening her lingerie drawer. She lifted a filmy peach nightgown to reveal the pistol lying in a nest of white lace.

"Mama, I hid that for your own good," I said.

"I know why you took it," she said. "That's why I let you get away with it. But let's get one thing straight, right here and right now."

I crossed my arms and leaned against the wall, waiting but defensive.

"I am the mother. You are the child. From tonight, we are going to start acting like we understand that again."

I remembered Maw Maw saying that Mama tried to control things to make herself feel safe. I'd be glad to let her run her own life again. I was bone-tired of trying.

"Nothing would make me happier, Mama."

"And stop worrying about me killing myself. It's not going to happen. Your father bought this pistol to protect us, and that's all it's going to do. There have been times I've wished I was dead, over the past few years. But I'm not about to try to do God's job for him. Understand?"

I nodded as an invisible weight the same size and shape as my mother slipped soundlessly from my shoulders. I felt light enough to fly and concentrated on keeping the bottoms of my feet connected to the floor.

She dipped her left hand into the pocket of her bathrobe, and in my mind's eye I saw Daddy's hand plunge deep into the pocket of his khaki fishing pants so long ago, on the day we made the cast net. Mama held her clenched fist out to me. "Take this."

I reached out my shaking hand to take what she offered, but her hand rested in mine, unopened. She stared at me, long and hard, her blue eyes glistening. "You think I hate you, because you washed your daddy's pajamas. You think I don't understand, that I can't forgive."

She waited until I murmured agreement. "I don't blame you, though. What I did was wrong. I didn't know how wrong until I'd done it and it couldn't be undone. I did it with the best of intentions, but I stole your only comfort, and once I realized that, there was no way to give it back. I am so, so sorry."

Her other hand grabbed my wrist, above my hand that still held her clenched fist.

"I wish you hadn't done it, but I know you did the best you could, the only thing you knew to do. When your Daddy died, I should have taken care of you, not the other way around. But all I could do for you then was to keep breathing in and out."

I could feel how slippery Mama's grip on any kind of happiness was. How could I help her hang on, after all she'd lost?

I thought of Suzie and her undying love for her own deeply flawed parents. *Forgive*, she whispered in my mind's eye.

"We both did the best we could, Mama."

I felt Mama's ragged breath as she struggled for self-control. I'd never loved her more than at that moment, when I realized how hard that damaged bird was fighting for her life. I wanted to ask her if she loved me. But then she opened her hand, and I didn't have to ask.

"I cut this from his pajama pocket for you," she said. "Sew it on your apron, to cover that scissor-hole."

She opened her hand in mine, and a wrinkled scrap of cool cotton fabric, robin's egg blue and light as a butterfly's wing, unfolded in my palm. I saw that it was heart-shaped, and lightly stained. With the tip of one finger, Mama smoothed its ragged edges.

"Honey, one thing your Daddy showed me is that a heart is not a pie that's cut into slices, with some slices larger or smaller than others. I loved my mother and father and brother with my whole heart. I loved my husband with my whole heart. I love *both* my children the same way."

Her grip tightened on my wrist. "Jimmy is my prodigal son. And when he comes home, we'll kill the fatted calf and celebrate with what's left of this family. But never doubt that I know who my good and steady child is."

Her blue eyes glistened.

"You are the very best thing in my life. You give me reason to live."

With those words, she gave me back my own chance for a happy, *normal* life—whatever that might turn out to mean.

My mother folded me in her arms, my father's heart pressed close between us. Then we sewed it on the apron, together.

Epilogue - 2005

My twenty-year-old daughter, Jessica, and I drove one Tuesday afternoon last May, from Orlando, where I was the book reviewer at the local newspaper by day and a poet by night, back home to Jacksonville for Maw Maw's funeral.

We pulled into Memorial Park for the graveside service, and found Mama standing with Kat, who had been her daughter-in-law for over twenty years. She and Jimmy had never had children of their own, so they lavished their parental instincts on their niece Jessica, and on Lucy's three boys. A slight limp was the only reminder of Kat's accident. Her dyslexia had been diagnosed and conquered long ago with the same determination that she'd used to learn to walk again. She was an accomplished painter, and they owned a gallery at Ponte Vedra Beach, where they sold her work alongside Jimmy's nature photographs.

We shared hugs all round and walked to the rows of chairs set up by the grave.

After the terrible year when she buried both her father and her husband, Mama seemed to get used to funerals. She almost began to enjoy them. At least it seemed that way to Jimmy and me.

"Nothing gets Mama going like a good funeral," my brother joked, looking around the cemetery to be sure his voice hadn't carried to the other mourners.

"I think they make her feel useful," I whispered back. "She certainly knows the drill." As if on cue, Mama helped a group of relatives move casseroles from one car's trunk to another, then supervised the placement of several beribboned floral sprays.

Mama had continued to take in strays, like she did with Suzannah. The last was Maw Maw, who was supposed to move in for a few months to recuperate from a minor stroke but ended up staying for fifteen years. She and Mama fussed and fought and loved one another until Maw Maw's death at age ninety.

We buried her next to Paw Paw, across from Daddy. I watched Mama, wondering if she felt bereft without Maw Maw's company, or relieved that the burden of her care was lifted. I decided it was probably a mixture of both.

Uncle Travis and Aunt Rita Faye arrived. They were old then, of course. Her raven-black hair had turned white, and she was blind, a side effect of all the shock treatments of her youth. I watched my uncle from afar, as he tenderly helped her navigate from their car, past the gravestones and tent-poles, to a seat of honor beside the casket.

As my life had gotten busier with a husband, child, and career, I had neglected keeping up with my relatives outside my nuclear family, so I was happy to see that each of the Harper children came to honor Maw Maw, except Suzannah, who, I heard, was traveling the world, still trying to find a happy home. As we stood in a cluster of cousins, sewing up the holes in our family history with gentle gossip before the burial, Suzie's sister Priscilla told Jessica and me that Suzie had gone through a couple of husbands, but that her third one seemed like a keeper. She'd had no children, Delilah confided, which was probably for the best. Suzie may have inherited more than just her mother's gorgeous eyes, Travis,

Jr. implied, without actually saying it. As I said before, such things are not stated directly, not in the Deep South.

"Bless her heart," Jessica murmured.

How sweetly each one of Uncle Travis and Aunt Rita Faye's children hugged and kissed their mother and father, there under the funeral tent. How joyously their littlest grandchildren ran among the headstones, oblivious that this was a place and time of solemnity. How courteously and appropriately their older grandchildren behaved, making their parents proud.

I approached Uncle Travis and embraced him after the funeral. I took Aunt Rita Faye's hand, as she sat beside my mother, told her who I was, and asked her how she was feeling. I told her she looked pretty in her new suit. I was able to be civil, even kind.

They asked about my latest poetry collection, and I promised to send them a copy as soon as I got back home. I wrote down their address and telephone number on the back of Maw Maw's funeral program, thinking back to the days when their ring was long-short-long on our party line.

As they walked away, I thought about the mistakes that parents and children make with each other, and how time dulls the pain of those mistakes, if we let it, and leaves the bonds intact.

I walked across the row to my father's grave, and stared down at the double marker at my feet, our family name in the middle, Daddy's first name on the left, Mama's on the right. On Daddy's side there were two dates, on Mama's, just one. Underneath them both it read, "Together Forever."

I didn't hear Mama approach until she slipped her arm through mine.

"Jessica just gave her cousins some interesting news, about her and Tina," she said.

I scanned her face, which was expressionless.

"I don't think she knew I was standing behind her."

"Did you have any idea, Mama? Are you shocked?"

"Oh, maybe an inkling, once in a while. She's always been so good at sports."

I grimaced. What a stereotype.

"I told her exactly what I thought," Mama said.

I peered around for Jessica. Was she upset? What kind of damage would I have to undo?

Mama raised her eyebrows, as if sharing a rich joke. "I told her I was pleased that she was happy in love. It's a rare thing when you meet your perfect mate."

I realized I'd been holding my breath. I exhaled, smiling. My mother never ceased to amaze me.

She gestured toward Daddy's grave. "He was a good man. I was lucky in love, and you were lucky to have him for a father."

I nodded. "I know. You got lucky twice, with husbands."

She smiled, and her gaze found her second husband, Bob, and her son Jimmy in the crowd. She squeezed my arm. "And twice more, with my children."

Mama opened her queen-sized purse, big enough to transport a baby or a small watermelon.

"I have something for you," she said.

One glance at the zig-zagged lavender edge told me what she'd brought me.

I took the memory apron from her eager hands. "Where did you find this?" I asked.

"In a box of old poetry books and such that you left downstairs in the garage when you married Chet," Mama said. "I've decided to start clearing out that mess under the house so it won't be such a burden on you kids when I pass on." She lowered her voice. "You wouldn't believe the racy sketch-book I found down there. At first I was afraid it had been your father's, but then Kat assured me it was hers, from some art history project she did years ago on pin-up girls. She and Jimmy took it to the gallery and put it in a display case. It's labeled *Not for Sale at Any Price*. Can you imagine?"

I smiled to think of Kat keeping her vow of secrecy so long, still protecting my father, who had once given her a second chance at life.

As Mama walked me to my car, away from the grave of the woman who'd helped raise us both, I tied the faded apron around my waist, thinking of my family, some related by blood, others the sisters of my heart; those gathered around me, and those who'd gone on before. As I looked at the little ones playing at my feet and considered those yet to come, I was sure of one thing.

Love is the miracle.

And however long we have each other, love is enough.